You're the Spitting Image of My Angel

Publishing-in-support-of,

EDUCREATION PUBLISHING

RZ 94, Sector - 6, Dwarka, New Delhi - 110075
Shubham Vihar, Mangla, Bilaspur, Chhattisgarh - 495001

Website: *www.educreation.in*

ISBN: 978-93-88719-97-1

Price: 150.00

Printed in India

You're the Spitting Image of My Angel

Abhijith D

Acknowledgment

Nothing in this word is a solo effort for a creation, neither this book. From the person who starts to print this book to the delivery executive who delivers it to the readers, shops, everyone has a particular role that I'd like to thank.

1) I would like to express my vote of thanks to my parents for their endless support and having faith in me. They are my first Guru's.

2) I' am thankful to my sister Tanisha who supported me and encouraged me from the start of this book and keeping me go even when am down.

3) I' am thankful to my uncle (Vasudevan) and aunt (Smitha Vasudevan) who kept me going when I had nothing and today here I 'am under their gracious blessings

4) I' am thankful to my friend (Yathish) for believing in me and being with me even during tough times

5) Thank you Priya Muniswamy (dolly) for selecting such a wonderful book cover for me. You have been a great help in my life and am grateful to have such a wonderful friend like you.

6) Thank you Rania for being with me and supporting me and you are one of a kind friend I wish everybody had.

7) Thank you Christina from Grammarly.com for helping me out getting back my novel when it was lost and without you I wouldn't have published this novel.

8) My sincere thanks to Sandeep who is a broher from another mother for helping me out researching a lot about Pathanamthitta district and sharing your love story as today the whole world is reading this.

9) Thank you Dr. Nikhil Chandwani for giving me tips and helping me out with my novel and under your guidance which I have achieved.

10) I' am also thankful to Educreation publishers for bringing out this novel "You're the spitting image of my angel." to the eyes of my fellow readers.

11) In the end am grateful to the God for helping me through this wonderful journey and help me face difficult obstacle for the person who I' am today.

SYNOPSIS

This is an Indian, Kerala based story of a poor guy called Rahul who falls in love with a beautiful girl Rahasya whereas she's from a middle-class family who's going to accept him but later she meets with an accident and loses her memory. Unaware of this, Rahul takes a step to his career and will fly to Australia.

Falling in love is very easy but facing rejection after proposing their feelings to their loved ones is very painful. After knowing about the incident Rahul starts all over again to fall in love and show the true feeling of love.
This story explains the struggle which Rahul goes through to win his love.

Welcome to ***"You are the spitting image of my angel"***. It's easy to fight to get what we want.
But is fighting an only option?
Will he bring back her memory?
Will he win her again?

PROLOGUE

Papa, It's time for the bed time story.
I'm tired baby, go sleep today.
I'll continue tomorrow.
But papa…………!
Stop, just go sleep, I yelled at her.

She banged the door and went inside crying.
Rahasya walks in from the kitchen.
Come on, baby, why are you ignoring her?
I didn't ignore her, I just said I'm tired.

Oh yeah! You are not tired of watching that match.
You better go and convince her or you are sleeping
on the couch, she said.

My mouth was wide open hearing her statement.
I went inside and she was crying.
Baby, cutie? Please don't cry.
Don't speak to me papa.
I laid down beside her.
My cutie, I'm going to tell you a story. Now stop
crying, I said.
She looked at me.
Really?
Yeah! Of course, I said.

ACT 1: Pathanamthitta

(1)

Pathanamthitta is a small district in Kerala where it's covered in dense forest and small towns are situated and developed in the here. This place is well known for the holy place Shabarimala, the place of lord Ayyappa. My name is Rahul and am from a poor family. I have been through a lot in my life like others. This is how my life went.
Here goes....

Kerala is known as God's own country, Some are born rich and some are born poor and am one of them who live to struggle burying my head in the ground for making money and taking responsibility for my family. My mother is a housewife, her name is Kamakshi and she does coolie work, as my father earns but spends all his money on drinking and he's an alcoholic. His name is Chandran. I have a brother who is studying. His name is Ranjith.
I don't speak with my father and brother.
My mother is my angel, She's everything to me.

It's been a long time since we used to walk like this, I said to Rudra.
We were in the middle of the forest where we had been to see the temple which was left behind as people could not visit the place due to wild animals.

The path to this place is dangerous.
From the main road, It's approximately 5 kms. Tall trees are there and while going inside we mark the trees with our machete so that we shouldn't forget our way out.
Once people go inside they don't come back at all. Only few people have returned.
Either they get eaten by the wolves or get stamped by the elephants and die. Only one in million come out.
The temple which is inside the forest is the border of the city limits. After that It's completely forest.

We can see Elephants drinking water by a small stream which flows through the middle of the forest and people take rifles or sword to defense themselves if they get caught by the wolves or elephants. Some carry crackers so that they can scare away the boars when they attack.
The weather was bad.

It seems like a storm is coming, Rudra said.
Yeah! We better run, I said.
It's not safe during these times in the forest.
What if we hide in the temple, He asked?
No, Rudra, It's not safe. I have seen people dying as the stones fell of their head. The safest place right now is to get out of the forest, I said.
We will go, he said.

As we were walking it began to rain suddenly and we ran as fast as we can.

We reached the main road and then followed the road to a to a nearby bus stop. By the time we got there, We were completely drenched. It was too cold and shivering, After all, it's God's own country. Suddenly four girls came laughing and cheering towards the bus stop drenched, My eyes naturally gazed at one of the girls.

As soon as I saw her my heart told she's the love of my life. My heart started to beat. I could literally hear the beat through my mouth. I was looking at her eyes so deeply I couldn't even hear what Rudra was speaking to me. Both her eyes twinkled like the stars in the night.

She wore a red chudidhar filled with black bottom. Her hair was long and she had a Chandana (*a bindi made out from sandalwood*) on her forehead, I stood there and suddenly I hear Rudra shouting at my ears telling that it stopped raining. As I started to move I looked back and caught her staring at me as if I murdered her whole family.

That single stare made my heart beat like an express and I moved on. Later that day Rudra dropped me at home and I slept on my bed outside the house in the front yard and kept looking at the sky thinking about her.

(2)

I overheard the girls speaking that they will come the next morning around 7:00 a.m, So I assumed that even she will be there. I went to sleep and woke up early in the morning thinking about her and I went there to see if she's come. I was searching her and then somebody patted on my back.
I turned back to see only her looking at me and asking me, who are you waiting for?
I was confused for a moment.
I said, am waiting for a bus.
She said okay in a doubtful manner.
She paused for a moment and then asked me, Did you come to see me or? and paused.
I was scared but still improvised telling, you? why?.

She was convinced by my answer and then she said I saw you here with your friend yesterday.
I said yeah! it was raining, and then immediately I asked what's your name?
Am Rahasya she said.

I paused for a moment looking at her. She waved her hands near my eyes and said Hello! Are you dreaming? I said no, I just want you to know that you have a wonderful name.
She smiled and rolled her hair back behind her ears which were so beautiful. I felt as if I saw an angel.

The bus came and she went on, Before leaving she looked at me and said, you seem like a good guy,

Meet me here at the same time tomorrow, I nodded my head with a smile, and again she put her head through the window and asked my name,
Raaaahul, I screamed.

After she left, I danced in the middle of the road with happiness and people started to laugh at me.

The next day, I went to the same place and she was wearing a bluish color Anarkali waiting for me. I saw her and said inside my mind, am stupid to make her wait.
I think your the only person who makes a girl wait she said, I smiled and said sorry. I couldn't take my eyes off her, such beautiful creations made by the god himself. Of course, Kerala girls are born beauties. People say that they are sent from heaven made by God himself.

After that, she gave me sweet and said take it, she had a grumpy face. Before taking the sweet I asked what happened, why are you so grumpy? am dressed like a queen, and am giving you sweets and you're still asking me? she asked?

I said, of course, it's your birthday. She smiled and that was a great escape. It was a wild guess.
I wished her and that day and it was September 17th.
That day we went to the temple, Aranmula Parthasarathy temple. It was approximately 25 KMS from Konni. It was Vishnu's temple. This is one of the famous temple in patthanamthitta. The

temple is built in such a way that from all four sides are made equally and It's the same design. Of course, those days engineers were filled with wonders. Nowadays we don't see such type of temple's anywhere.

The largest boat race in India is held here. This is one of the ancient shrines in the town.

It is said that when the ornaments Ayyappa wear are brought from the Pandhalam and this is one of the temple they stop before reaching Shabarimala.

I sat down and spoke a lot of things.

What is your dream, she asked me?

I got so many dreams like,

Go abroad, earn money, buy cars, bikes, become rich, construct a house here in our place, buy my parents what all they deserve. I want to get settled in New Zealand. I don't want a high profile. I'll live peacefully with a low profile status, I said.

What about me, she asked?

Of course, Am going to be with you. After everything if I don't have you then there is no meaning of life, I said.

Her eyes filled with tears. She hugged me in public. I was so damn scared. In Kerala they don't entertain hugs and they charge us with obscene acts in public and will be behind bars. I started to shiver. I whispered, Rahasya, people are watching. She looked at me straight into eyes.

Nobody can touch us Rahul. You are mine forever, she said.

Suddenly her mom called her and she was like be quiet.

I looked at her face and she was saying *"Sheri ma, vara ma".* (Okay mother, I'll come) After that, I asked her who is that? It's my mother she said.

I asked about her parents and she showed their pictures on her mobile. She was from a middle-class family who's trying to lead the life balanced. Her father was wearing a white mundu (*a kind of dhoti which is worn around the waist in Kerala*) and a shirt, and he was posing for the photo with eyes wide open definitely looked like a terminator from the future.

Her mother was posing with her eyes half shut and I felt like am seeing a sloth whose having sleepless nights. The love of my life had a freak family.

She was the only daughter. She stayed 15km apart from my home in a place called Aruvapulam and am living in Konni. We both are from the same district Pathanamthitta. That day we exchanged our numbers and went back to the house.

(3)

After exchanging numbers every day I used to chat with her, I wouldn't even have dinner without her. I loved her so badly, but I was so scared to tell her. Each and every day was like a blooming flower, I felt like she's everything to me.

My friends told she's fake, some of her friends told she's not good. I didn't care for all those. I didn't have the money or luxurious stuff to take her with but all I had was love. After a month on October 7th around 09:30 pm, I texted her. she was awake.

I gave a long pause and I said I love you. I didn't receive any reply from her end. I called her and asked what happened. I need time she said, I said okay, take your own time, I'll call you by 7:00 in the morning.

Think a million times before you take a decision. she just said hmm and hung up the phone.

I could literally feel the disappointment she felt because of me. I felt happy but at the same time, I was scared of what she would give me a reply in the morning. That particular night I couldn't sleep properly.

The next day I woke up and it was October 8th at 7:05 a.m, without brushing my teeth I called her and for the first ring, she didn't attend my call. I was scared and shivering. I kept my finger on the call button thinking whether to call her again or not, I started to sweat, I called her again. And this time as soon as the call went she attended my call and said you're late. I said hmm.

Did you have your breakfast I asked her? I love you too Rahul she said. My ears started to ring like a bell. At first, I was not sure of what she said, Then again I asked and she said the same thing.

I started to jump in front of my house, My mom was shouting at me telling what the hell's going on there, you dirty idiot.

Go fresh up soon, I have made breakfast said, mom. After that, I went up and brushed my teeth, took a shower, had my breakfast and combed my hair and went running towards the bus stop to see her. As I waited I saw Rudra with his new bike.
He saw me and told it's his new bike, just got delivered from the showroom, and seeing that I was excited because it's my favorite bike too.

It was NS pulsar 200 ccs. That day I decided to own a bike. It's hard to afford such an expensive bike. But it's not impossible.

I saw her coming. She saw me and was blushing. We planned to bunk the college and go to Konni elephant reserve.

It's a famous reserve, The view of elephants standing together in hundred's are mind-blowing.

Since the ancient times Konni is famous for elephant training. The elephants are captured from the dense forests of the Western Ghats and then they are brought to the elephant training cage at Konni.

This place is called as "Anakoodu"

After all, Konni is known for its elephant cages, forests, and rubber plantations.

The trainers start to train the elephants with the help of tamed elephants. People who go there can get a close look at the elephants and also people can see the mischievous behavior of the baby elephants.

We spent a lot of time there and took dozens of selfies.

By the time it was late so we had returned home and started to chat, I have something to tell, she said. I called her up and asked what happened, Don't be sad, She said. I asked her to tell me. She said that she's going to Kochi regarding her college training camp.

At first, I felt sad but then It's a good news. I told please go ahead, This might bring you a placement in the future for your work. All the best I said. I used to work here and there for time being, works like wiring, catering, chopping woods in the forest for the city, construction work, in fact, I used to wash rich people's car to earn some money and surprise my mom.

I studied diploma in radiology and I used to work in the hospital where I used to earn 6,000/- per month.

I was thinking all these when she said she's leaving town, but I was happy. The next day I went her to drop off the bus stop and sent her. I felt lonely but still, had her in calls and chat all the time, two days passed by, I went to Meen Mutti waterfalls. This beauty is situated in Kallelli, in Waynad. Its approximately 100 KMS from Konni.

It's the second tallest falls in India. Most of the tourist places come there to relax. There are rock climbing, The nature's reserve will calm up any stressed up mind. It's a must and should visiting place for those who stay in India and even a lot of outsiders visit this place to enjoy. I sat near to the falls on a rock and started to think.

Am earning here just 6,000/- from what I studied, so if I go to cities, I have may have a chance to earn good money, and also go abroad.

Once upon a time I had a good friend in Bangalore. His name is Krissh, His mother was working in a reputed diagnostic company as a manager. I thought that I can call him up and ask for help.

It was a long time that I spoke to him. He had helped with a lot of stuff. I was sure that there will be some way to succeed this.

(4)

How are you? I said. Hey, am good buddy Krissh replied? Long time no see? he asked.
I laughed and I need help from you, I said. What's the favor? he asked me.
I want a job in a medical facility, I said.

What's your qualification he asked me? Diploma in radiology, I said.
He asked me to come to Bangalore and then let's talk about it.

Soon I packed all my bags and the following day I said to mom that am leaving town and going to Bangalore to search a new job. I traveled from Pathanamthitta to Bangalore on a bus and reached Bangalore.

Well a lot of people know about Bangalore, total chaos, traffic, pollution, minor accidents are normal in Bangalore. Bangalore is a place where a poor man becomes rich and a rich man will start to beg within months. Sometimes people call the city that never sleeps.

Well, I reached a place called Halasuru. I called him up and he came to pick me up in a Honda activa. He invited me home and offered me tea with some snacks. I was thankful to him. I freshened up myself and called Rahasya, She was about to have dinner. How are you? she asked me. I said am good, and I want to tell you something. Tell me she said. I'm in Bangalore, I said.

She hung my call immediately. I called her up again and said, am sorry. I know that I didn't inform you. I came here for a job and am staying in one of my friend's home, I said. Please keep me informed always, She said. Definitely, I said. After that the next day we went to Aarthi diagnostics, and I gave my resume, Krissh was with me the whole time.

He spoke to the following authorities to find me a job. Since Bangalore is the capital of Karnataka. All the people speak Kannada and it's the state language, The only problem with me was I didn't know the language. All I ever spoke in Kannada was 'Kannada Gottila' means I don't know Kannada.

It's a shame to tell like that being in Karnataka. Krissh helped me a lot, And I don't know what to do to get a job. I applied over 10 Medical facilities and all the companies rejected me.
We tried even with Krissh's mother's company and they said I need even more experience.
I was frustrated. My disadvantage in Bangalore was I don't speak Kannada.
We roamed here and there all over Bangalore for about 17 days. We walked a lot saving the bus fare for xerox copies of my resume. I almost gave up but Krissh had hopes.

He didn't give up no matter how many times I got rejected. He contacted his mentor who helped him in his education. Somehow Krissh's mother spoke with him and he gave a job and also a room to stay with three times food.

I was thankful to Krissh. I had no words but hug him. Later after that, I called up mom and said this good news, She was happy. I called up Rahasya, I got a job, I said. She started to jump in joy, I can hear her scream throughout her room.

(5)

A month passed by, I received my first salary. It was 12,000/-. The double what I was earning in my hometown. I called up mom and said I received the salary. Amma was happy to hear that I was earning so much.

I called up Rahasya and said about this, She was happy to hear, And the next day I went to Krissh's home, And Krissh has a baby sister, Her name is Tanisha. Krissh calls her Minnu. She's studying in 7th standard and she's fond of pizzas. So I went to Domino's center and ordered a chicken sausage, golden corn Pizza mania, It cost me around 250 bucks. I went home and gave that.

Minnu jumped up and grabbed it telling thank you 'etta' (which means brother in Malayalam). Krissh looked at my Face and Krissh's mother doesn't treat me like a stranger.

She treats me like her own son. She told to come home every weekend and enjoy some time with us. In the middle of this, I keep getting calls from Rahasya, Minnu saw this and got suspicious, She keeps asking me who is that and I used to tell her she's my friend.

Krissh saw her name once and he said somebody's calling you. He's suspicious of me but he never asked me, Most of the time he pretended not to be suspicious and goes away.

One fine day she called me and immediately I said to Krissh that, I want to tell you something'. Tell me, he replied. I said, let me speak first and then I'll tell you. He walked with me as I spoke to her. She asked me how was I doing? Am good, I replied. We were talking about my work and environment, colleagues etc.

After that, I hung up the phone and then turned towards Krissh. He smiled at me and I said yes, I do have a small love story. I know, Krissh replied. I can tell easily when a person is in love, he said. Well, it's going on for four months, I said.

He looked at me and raised his eyebrows giving me an awkward expression. Why what happened I asked him? Nothing, you told it's from four months so I was surprised that your love is so strong by now, he said.

I laughed at him and said how I proposed my feelings to her, And how she accepted.
I'll tell you something, don't get offended he said.
You are from a poor family, Your busy making money and how come you have time for love, he asked? Love is something which doesn't ask permission before coming, I said. He gave a wicked laugh, his laugh was indirectly telling me I will suffer.

I will not suffer, I said. He laughed again, and said come on bro, I didn't mean like that. After that, he took me to a chat shop and bought me a masala puri and he bought himself a bhelpuri. And he started to advise me about love.
I don't know why he was advising me but I guess he felt something wrong with me. Love is something which is the most powerful feeling that earth have, Nobody can defeat love. Some play with love, some take love seriously and if they get broke they attempt suicide, some will never have love but later they fall in love.

Some are there who uses Love for sex. What type of love is yours, he asked? I was surprised he knew so much about love. Because he's three years younger to me and already knows so many about love and life. I had a doubt about him whether he had his own love his story or is he in love?

My mind was gathered with thoughts, Yet I didn't ask him. And that night, we watched a movie together. Krissh was always a Hollywood guy, He used to watch only English movies, And am just the opposite one, I do watch English, but most of the time I stick to Tamil and Malayalam movies. The next day was Sunday, I got back to work and then as usual days started to run as fast as a train.

Krissh had a good habit, He never smokes or drinks. And when I ask why? He used to say that when he dies, he wants to donate his organs for free.

Such a good person he was, He used to sit alone and listen to songs and had a craze of getting into the film industry, He usually makes songs, music, short comedy episodes, albums, he writes novels too. He's a good singer too. In fact, he was already in the film industry. He's also a good dancer.

Kind of all-around celebrity, He had little fans in social media, Facebook, Instagram, Twitter, Youtube etc. He was a good guy.

His attitude made girls fall in love but he never accepts them when proposals come, Instead, he will tell let's be good friends and enjoy their company.

Earlier I said he had no friends, That's true. But he had a lot of girlfriends, Hence he got the name, Krishna.
He followed one rule in his life, He never trusts anybody.

(6)

Few days after I got a call from home telling that mom's sick. I had to rush immediately, I didn't inform Krissh, I couldn't inform Rahasya too. I went home and saw my mom laying down on the bed, As soon as she saw me she woke up and hugged me. How is work? How is Bangalore? How is Krissh? she asked. All types of questions she was asking, Did you eat? she said. Amma? you leave all that, How are you? I said. Am fine, but little fever. It will go soon, she said.

Soon I bought her medicines and gave her and then by three days she was fine. I returned to Bangalore and came back to work, I got a call, It was Rahasya.

I received the call, How are you Ammu? I said.
She was crying.
What happened? I said. I miss you, I want to see you soon, She said.
I miss you too Ammu, I said.
One day I'll take an off and come to Kochi, I said.
Really? she asked.
Of course Rahasya I said.

It was time for me to take care of patients in the Operation theatre department, So I hung up the call and ran to O.T.

Krissh called me, What happened Rahul bro?

You didn't come this week he said. Am very sorry Krissh. I had been to hometown as mom was sick. It was a sudden plan, So I ran over there to check out things, I said.
Oh! Don't worry brother I didn't know, He said.

Later that week was so busy I didn't get enough sleep. Day and night all together they put me in shifts and I started to rest down my head on the X-ray table only. After that week, I went to Krissh house and slept nicely.

He spent almost all the nights by writing lyrics, sometimes novels and sometimes Hollywood movies.

The next day the manager of the hospital approached me. Wonderful job Rahul, He said.
I was puzzled to see him praising my name, but at the same time, I was scared whether I did something wrong.

He was happy regarding my hard work, So he gave me 5 days off. I was so happy that he gave me a small vacation so that I can go to Kochi to meet her. Immediately I called Rahasya. Ammu, am coming to see you next week. My manager gave me 5 days off.

Be ready to meet me. She was jumping and screaming with joy. After that, I called Krissh.
Yes? Krissh speaking, He said.

Of course, it was the hospital telephone so he didn't save the number. Krissh, It's Rahul, Am calling from hospital telephone, I said.
Tell me, He said. Am leaving for Kochi next week to see Rahasya, I said.
Did you get leave approval, Krissh asked me? I forgot to tell you, My manager gave me off for 5 days because of my hard work, After all, that's what he said, I said.

Well, that's good news, he said. Be careful when you go there, Don't be in trouble, He said.
I laughed out loud, If I get in trouble I will call you, I said. He laughed at my poor joke and then I hung up.
The following week I booked a bus to Kochi from Bangalore.
I reached Kochi by morning at 06:15 a.m approximately.

ACT 3: Kochi

(7)

Hello Rahasya, I said. Where are you? she asked me. Am in front of your hospital I said.
What took you so long, She said.
I took a room here and then freshened up myself, Didn't have breakfast, Just tea.
Now am waiting for you so that I can have breakfast with you.
She laughed and said she's coming down. I observed that Kochi is a bit like Bangalore, The city is so expensive in everything. I can see girls wear short skirt and shorts in the city.
It's like M.G.road in Bangalore. Metro pillars were placed and it was under construction. Lulu mall was the second biggest mall in Asia and the largest mall in India.

Everywhere buildings and traffic, Minor fights were common in Kochi because of minor accidents happen due to traffic. Finally, she came down and she ran to me and gave a warm tight hug.

It felt so good. I was so hungry that I could eat her. Come on Ammu, Let's eat, I said. Let's go near Lulu mall.
I know a place where nice idly's and dosas are served, She said.

Lulu mall was just half a km from her place. We walked and then there was this nice hotel, Hot dosas were served with chutney.
Such a nice feeling to eat when a person is most hungry, My eyes were closed with the first bite and my expression was like the dairy milk silk add's.

Don't you get good food in Bangalore? She asked.
It's good, but all are in Karnataka style, I said.
She gave a fake laugh as if she's enjoying here with her hostel food.
After that, we went to Lulu Mall. It was so huge that one must need 3 days to complete the mall tour. It's a confusing mall.
We went together to a Malayalam movie. After that, We went to the beach. We had ice cream, and also some popcorn.

We sat on the beach and started to hold hands and she put her head on my shoulder.
How much do you love me, Rahul? she asked.
I looked at her face.
How much do you think I love you? I said.
She looked at me and smiled. What a question baby? she said.
Well, I love you as much as I love my mom, I said.
She hugged me then and there only and she gave me a kiss. It was exactly the sunset, And our kiss completed the day.

From behind a cop saw this. His mustache was so big that we can't even see his lips. He came towards us like the villain in movies.

He was screaming at us for the obscene act and
Ammu hid behind me and she said to give him
some money and send off.
He asked to come to the station, And I took a 50
rupee note and still, he was shouting.

Ammu started to laugh. Give 100/-, He will go, She
said. I took a 100 rupee note and he took the 50 and
100 together and he was like beware, Don't do such
stuff here.

Okay sir, I said. And he left. Money plays
everything in the country, no matter what you are.
Ammu started laughing loudly. Why are you
laughing, I asked her.
You lost that 50 and 100 together, She said and
started to laugh.
I chased her down the beach laughing together.

(8)

Then I took her to my room, Of course, She informed her roommates that she wants to stay with me for the next 5 days. Please tell the warden that am working night shifts, She said to her roommates. They were all teasing her and she hung the phone with a cute smile.

The following night I ordered pepper chicken fry. She loves pepper chicken and tandoori a lot. So the room service came and he gave one half pepper chicken fry and one full tandoori.

As I bought two together he served a complimentary dessert DBC (Death by chocolate) ice cream. It was a small bucket filled with black forest cake and thick dark chocolate toppings with dry fruits and hot chocolate sauce. The ice cream was kind of hot and cold. And with chicken, I ordered a biriyani. Then we had Biriyani and chicken and after that, She had ice cream.

I wasn't interested in the ice cream because I had a cold. After that, I laid down on the bed and started to watch tv. She went to the washroom and then she came and laid next to me. She put her head on my shoulders. And she was trying to bite my ears. Why are you biting me? I said. She started to bite my neck. Why Ammu? I said.

Don't you feel anything? she asked.

It pains dumbo, I said.

You are a total idiot Rahul, She said.

Arrey! it's paining when you bite me, After all, you are a human Ammu, I said.

She stood up and put her hand on her forehead.

Rahul, When a girl is biting or trying to kiss a man's neck then it means she wants something, She said.

I was a stupid guy, I was not understanding what she was trying to tell me.

What are you trying to tell me Ammu, I said.

You are the dumbest man I've ever see on the face of the earth, She said.

Am sleepy Ammu, And I don't understand your riddles, I said.

She slapped me on my face slowly. Come on remove your dress, She said.

I was so scared and surprised at what I've heard. I asked her again, And she said the same. What do you want to do Ammu? I asked.

She smiled by showing all 32 teeth. Come on Rahul, I want to do it, She said. Ammu, It's dangerous, I said.

What's dangerous is there in that, She said.

To be honest I was scared as hell to do it. Arrey, dumbo! remove, She said and forced me to remove my robe.

It was my first time. Our mouths started to explore each other. My tongue was inside her mouth. Warm breath of her was feeling on my neck. Finally, at

last, we made it out. We had a good night sleep. The next day she went to work and took a half day and came back. As usual, The days went on. We had lots of fun during these 5 days.
Kochi was one of the most beautiful memories of my life.

Soon I came back from Kochi.

As I had travelled back from Kochi, I received missed calls but I didn't have balance to call back.

(Rahasya was crossing the road. She was thinking of Rahul.
A car had hit her and she was down in the middle of the road.
She was lying there in the pool of blood.
People gathered around and one of her friend recognized her and she helped her reach the hospital. Soon the situation was communicate to Krissh.)
All these were never known to Rahul

(9)

Krissh called me. How are you? How was your trip? How is Rahasya? Altogether he said this.

I didn't know what to tell, What not to tell. I was mixed up on my trip and traveling. But there was some unusual feeling in his voice. I was scared, All types of thoughts started to flow in my mind. At first, I thought there might be some issue in the workplace.

What happened? I said. No, Rahul, There's actually a good news for you, I said.
Come soon to my home after work. I'll tell you, I said. I hate surprises, He said.

I laughed at him and hung the phone. I had been to his house. What's the surprise, I asked? Krissh gave me some letter.
It was in an envelope and on top, It said "transfer to Australia". I opened the letter and saw.
It said, " Dear Rahul, with immediate effect you are appointed as the HOD of Radiology department and transferred to Canberra with accommodations and service".

The rest of the letter contained my work and payments. I sat there immediately and started crying. It was a dream come true. I never expected

this to happen. I hugged Krissh so badly, He started
to tap my back. My tickets were booked on January
15th, and my presence was needed in Australia on
the 17th of January.

I informed my mother and went to native to take her
blessings, I came back to Bangalore and then
packed up all my stuff for the journey.
Krissh and his mother came with me to Devanahalli
international airport.

Krissh hugged me once more at the doorway of the
airport, I cried so badly that I almost felt like
leaving my family away and going. I had to go for
the passport and visa check and then my security
check along with baggage. And then I needed to
board the flight at gate 3. After my security check,
there was an hour left for taking off. I waited in the
waiting area where the gate was just behind me and
I could see my airlift in the window from the place.

I wanted to inform my darling. But as I was
overjoyed I forgot to tell her. I called her up from
the waiting area to tell her.
She never received the call.

I tried 20 times She didn't pick. I was worried.
Immediately after 2 minutes, received a message
telling she's busy. I wanted to surprise her, As she
sent she's busy I thought she was stuck up in some
work and I became quiet.
My time was up, I walked to the gate as they
announced that my flight is going to departure. I

entered the gate, The gate from the airport to flight was kind of a rectangular tunnel.

As I approached I saw a beautiful air hostess welcoming me. I made a namaskar gesture and went inside.

It was a huge flight, Emirates. It was a 16-hour journey from Bangalore to Australia, connecting from Singapore. That way I thought am lucky to see only the view of Singapore from the flight.
The seat was comfy, First class. Seat belts signs were on and the air hostess was waving at the people about safety and procedures.

The feel of the engine pulled me back to the seat and as the flight ascended I saw the view of Bangalore becoming smaller and smaller until we disappeared into thick clouds.

(10)

Ah! the atmosphere of Canberra was so damn hot. Of course, Australia is the smallest country, as well as a continent in the world and 80% of the continent, is deserted and the country is well known for wool production.

I was so tired. Air hostess faces were happy and energetic as the first time I saw them in Bangalore and also in Singapore. They started to thank us for flying with them.

As soon as I walked out the gate they started to check the passport by the immigration department. I got a green seal from them and I guess they don't like Indians.

Staffs in the airports started to make faces at me and even a cop started to check me asking me if I carried anything unusual.

I felt really bad about this but satisfied myself with a chocolate milkshake at the airport.

I met a Singh there. After all, it's a happy thing to see an Indian in foreign countries. No matter what they speak, India means such a mind relaxing. I didn't know Hindi, I spoke with him in English. He told he lived there in Australia and he just arrived from New Zealand as he went there to take care of some business.

He told me about his work, family, and where he lived. We exchanged numbers.

Then I took a cab outside the airport to the hospital. "Calvary John James hospital" It's located at 173, Strickland Cres, Deakin Act 2600.
It was a 15 minutes drive from the airport. I sat in the cab. And for the first time, I saw the cleanliness of the city. It was clean, tidy and tall skyscrapers can be seen, And also the traffic rules was so good that if the vehicles bump each other, they don't even fight. They just wait calmly for the cops to arrive and then sort it out with insurances. But India is famous for Sanskrit dialogues.
One can always hear Sanskrit in everyday life.

Soon I arrived at the hospital.

The front receptionist said, How may I help you, sir? Her accent was like the flow of the river in the dense forest.
Am a recruit transferred from India to the radiology department, I said.
Mr. Rahul, right? she said.
Yes, madam, I said. Heartly welcome to Strickland Cres, She said. I felt like Mr. Vijay (Illayathalapathi) in Mersal movie as his welcome was greater than mine.

Please sit down sir, She said. I sat down and was watching nature. There was a water fountain outside covered with flowers around, The sky was blue in color and no clouds, It was so hot. AC was provided so I didn't feel the heat.

There was a tv on and the national geographic channel was running. A man in a suit approached me, He was tall and fair. How are you, Mr. Rahul? he said. Am doing good sir, I said. Am Bruce. Am the managing director of this company, He said.

Come with me Rahul, He said. He took me to his chamber and said me to take a seat. He offered me a cup of coffee.

Cream or without cream? he said. I thought who the hell will put a cream into coffee, Without cream, I said. And all I got was a black coffee.
I looked at it. What happened Rahul, he said. Dear sir, This is black coffee, I said.
That's why I asked you cream or without cream, He said. And then I came to know what was the meaning of cream. I smiled at him and said, Thank you.

Sir, Am grateful. We had a good telepathy, He understood why I smiled.
First, He told me about the hospital. Let's take a stroll through the hospital.

He said. He introduced me to the radiology department and I found two of them were Indians and I was happy to meet them.
He then showed me my room. It was just behind the hospital. It was such a beautiful room.

AC, wifi, tv, refrigerator, bathtub, etc.
Everything was there. I felt like home.

It was just me alone. It was perfect. I thanked him.
Take rest, Enjoy a little bit of champagne. And hey
I forgot to tell your package.

You will be paid A$17,560.72 per annum, He said.
Just seventeen thousand? I said. What are you
talking about? He said. Buddy, according to the
Indian rupees you will be earning 9,60,000 for a
year and you will be earning A$1,560.87 cents for a
month that's 80,000/- just a month, He said.

After hearing the first part I fell down unconscious.
I came to conscious after 10 minutes in the hospital
ward with the MD next to me.

What happened buddy? Are you alright? He said.
Am really sorry sir, I have never earned that amount
of money ever in my life, I said. Come on man,
Cheer up. This is Canberra city, He said.
I have an emergency meeting, He said and left.

Later, I went to my room and opened the
refrigerator and poured myself a drink. Switched on
the tv and put HBO channel and passed my time till
evening.

(11)

How are you amma? I said on the phone. She was terrified as I forgot to call her after I reached Australia. When did you reach? how is the country? did you eat? All these questions were asked continuously by mom. Amma, Don't worry. Am fine. Country's good, I had a warm welcome.

I met the MD. He's a good person. He showed me to my room, I feel like am home amma, I said. It was evening and the time was 05:30 pm.
What's the time there right now amma, I said. It's 11:00 pm dear, Said amma.
There is an approximate of 5 and a half hours of time difference amma, I said.
I know Rahul, You eat good, Don't suffer, Be happy, She said.

I hung up the phone and then came to the balcony. The view of Australia in the night was extraordinary. All those lights and fewer people. All I could see on the roads were sports cars. I never found anybody riding in two-wheelers. Mcdonalds and pizza hut's delivery vehicles were Corolla Altis.

Toyota Innova and Honda company's cars were used as cabs. And if people were using motorcycles then I could see a big fat man with beards like a rock star going in groups or they are also called as bikers and they used Harley Davidson.

Some used Sports vehicles like Kawasaki brands and all were superbikes and they also used to be together. I never saw a single mileage giving bike's as we see in India. Australia was totally advanced.

I called Rahasya, There was no answer. I began to worry a little because I haven't spoken to her since I boarded the flight.
I tried again but still no answer.
I dropped messages such as call me back as soon as you get back. Well, as I was enjoying the view I got a call from an unknown number.
I answered and I heard somebody screaming help me, The accent was in Australian English.
I couldn't recognize who it was. Please come to the hospital ward, My son is bleeding, There are no doctors here, Please help me, These were the messages what I've heard.

Immediately I ran towards the hospital. A boy around 15 was hit by a car and his skull was fractured and the bleeding was severe.

I called a surgeon immediately, We have a skull fractured case, It's a boy in his 15, sir, It needs to be cauterized immediately, I said. When I had come to hospital from the airport and waited in the office, I had noticed the doctor's contact list books.

I saved the most important numbers on my mobile if I need in the case of emergency, So that way I had his number. Am on my way, He said. Within 5 minutes he arrived and immediately he took the boy to operation theatre and after 20 minutes he came. Who called me on my phone? he said.

I was sitting with his mother and convincing that he will be fine. The receptionist pointed towards me. Well done young man.

I want everybody to give a round of applause to this young man here, He said. Who is the mother of the patient, He said?
Yes doctor, With tears rolling down her eyes, She said. No need to worry.
He's perfectly alright. And don't pay the bill, This is on me, If you would have been 5 minutes late then it would have become a disaster, He said.
How did you get my number and what made you call me immediately at the right time Mr? He said.
Rahul sir, I said.

Ah! yes, Rahul, He said. I told him how I got his number when I reached the hospital and from then onwards he became a close friend.

Why she's not picking my call? I said to myself. Did she ditch me? No, That can't happen.

Hi krissh! How are you? Am doing good buddy, He said. Brother, I need a help, I said.
Tell me, He said. Rahasya is not answering my calls. It's been almost two weeks, I said.

Well, I'll check on her, He said. Please, Krissh. Ask her what I did? I don't want to lose her, I said. Don't worry Rahul, I'll check on her, He said. How are amma and appa? I said.

They are always awesome buddy, He said. I hung the phone after the conversation.

(12)

It was Friday night, First time in my life, I felt to go for a long drive. I asked my doctor that I wanted his car. He gave me, I went slowly along the freeway to the Lanyon homestead.

It was located on the outskirts of Canberra. It was a lonely place where sheep and cows were tied up, People around there called that part, The countryside. It was night and I stopped at the Lanyon cafe.

Ordered a cup of hot chocolate and cheeseburger and slowly listened to the music which played at the cafe. That day they conducted a small party, So people around there asked me to join.

They put up the disco lights and soon Cakes, burgers, drinks etc all types of food and then a dance floor was arranged.

All were dancing and among them, one girl asked me to dance with her. She was fair, She had blonde hair, She wore jeans and a top with a sweater over,

She was like an angel. I stood up and I was amazed as a girl is asking me to dance, Of course, am not that handsome.

She smiled at me, Well, your not that good dancer,
She said. I laughed, Yeah! Am not a good dancer.
By the way, come let's have a drink, I said.
She looked straight at me. It was an embarrassing
look. Drinks on me, I said.

We had two beers, I bought us a dinner. Is this a
date? She said. Nah! I already have a girl, Am
committed dear, I said.
Oh! who is that wonderful angel? She said.
Ah! she's from India and also she's there.
I don't know what's happened but she isn't
answering my calls, I said. Well, Ms. I paused.
Isabella, She said.
What is your good name? She asked? Rahul, I said.

You bought me dinner and we are having a
wonderful conversation and yet we didn't even
introduce ourselves, She said.

Yeah! I noticed that a moment ago, I said. We
laughed together and it was almost 02:30 am. I was
about to leave. Do you want to stay over, I mean I
don't mind having a guy around like you.
In fact, you are the first person am inviting over,
She said. I will look at her in silence. Alright, I can
come over, I said.

She took me to a nearby place where she stayed.
The house was awesome, It was made up of wood.
She stayed in the countryside. She had a dog, His
name is Nike.

As we entered inside, He stood there at the entrance and started barking at me. Nike, She said. He went inside. Come in Rahul, She said. I went inside. There was a big t.v, Then two bedrooms and all the furniture a family needs.

Where are your mom and dad? I said. She smiled, They are sleeping at the back of the house, She said. What are they doing for a living? I said.
Well, They don't need to do anything. They just sleep all day and night now, She said.
Oh, come on, you are kidding me right, I said.
Come on, I'll show you where they are asleep, She said.

She took me to the back of her house to see two grave lying down together. I was shocked to see that. I'm sorry, I didn't know, I said. It's okay Rahul. Take rest, You are tired and exhausted. If you need anything just call me, She said.

She offered me blankets, night dress, And a towel for my shower. I enjoyed her hospitality. Early morning she brought us coffee.

(13)

Wake up wake up sleepy head, She said. I woke up, took a shower. Do you know any tourist spots here, I said. Yeah! I actually wanted to ask you that do you have any plans to get out from here, She said.

Am actually an aerobics teacher and also a school teacher. My hobbies are exploring places, Enjoying around with Nike.

Am an artist too. Well, not a professional one, She said. I laughed at her. But still, you do all these kinds of stuff. I'm kind of a workaholic.

By the way, Are you planning to go now? She said. Yeah! I said. Well, Then do you wanna use my car or your car? She said.

Actually, it's not my car. It's my doctor's car, I said.
Let's take my car.
It's big, Spacious and also good for mountain areas, She said. Alright whatever you say, Isabelle, I said.

We sat in the car and she drove. Damn! she drove fast, I thought to myself.

We stopped by a place for breakfast, We had Coffee with cream and two egg cheeseburgers, Well am a hungry man. So I ordered another burrito. She was laughing at me seeing the way I eat. After that It was a long way, We filled up gas and from the

station, I brought us some chips and drinks. I drove for some time as she was tired. We reached a beautiful spot. There was a waterfall and the water was blue in color.
It was kind of an oasis in the middle of the desert. I parked her vehicle and then took all the camping stuff.

Hey Rahul! how are you, buddy? Krissh said. I'm doing good brother, I said. Krissh, She's still mad at me? I said. No brother, Why do you think like that? He said. Where are you? He said.

It's Saturday, So I thought that I can go for a long drive. I took the doctor's car and have come across a long way from the city with one of my friends.

She's a good person bro, I said. She? Who is that new friend bro? He said. I told the whole story of how I met her. That's a lovely story bro, He said.

Later, We went fishing and brought us some fishes and Isabelle new to live in the wild, So we made a bonfire and cooked us some food and stayed over the night at the pool. But the problem was mosquitoes.

They were bigger and not like Indian mosquitoes. We made up our own mini tents and separately.

Actually, It was one of the most memorable ones in my life. The next morning Isabelle and I went for a walk, Kind of a jog. It was fun. She was a good artist, So I often saw her drawing roughly on her mini pad or a notebook.

She used to talk a lot about nature, birds, wild animals etc. She loves animals more than herself. We went trekking together. It was so good but thirst killed me now and then.

Then we came back and the day just passed on like that. It was Sunday and we came back all the way to her place. I was totally tired so she was the one who drove us back. Once we reached.

She took me to the same old cafe and brought me drinks. Even she had some beer. In the evening I had to leave. So I bid goodbye and exchanged phone numbers and moved on. She was a wonderful friend who made my day.

(14)

That's a wonderful job bringing back my car in one piece, Said the doctor. I laughed at him.

Come on doctor, You can trust me, I said. I know Rahul but still, It was the first time I gave it to you not knowing whether you can drive or not and after all this is Australia.

Rules and regulations are very strict here, He said.
Yeah, sir, I noticed that here.
Well, your back after a refreshing weekend, Let's get to work, He said.

As I was in the x-ray room I called continuously to Rahasya. She never answered my calls. I dropped many messages, I called her number of times, again and again, She never returned or called me again. I was frustrated. At first, I thought she was playing but then I began to worry. I tried to call her mother but even her phone was switched off.

After many times of trying I called Krissh. What's up, bro? He said. Krissh,

She's not picking my calls, Her mother's phone is switched off. It's already been a month, I'm scared Krissh, I said.
Well, Rahul, I need to tell you something.
I didn't mean this to happen. I'm coming to Australia next month, Krissh said.

Tell me what happened, I shouted. I'll come here and explain to you.

Please until that don't ask Rahul, He said and hung up the phone. My day was wrecked up, My room was messed up. I had a rough day.

I didn't sleep properly, I knew something went wrong with Rahasya. But I didn't know what had happened. I didn't have my food in proper time. I was depressed.

I called Isabelle and told what had happened and she convinced me.
I felt so empty without her, I realized how important she is and how much I loved her.
I tried again and again just to speak with her but all my calls were unanswered.

I got a phone call from Krissh. Hello Rahul, I boarded the flight and I'll be landing tomorrow at the airport. Come to pick me, brother, He said.

I'll be waiting there at the entrance brother.
Come soon, I said. Security checks are going on now, I'll make a move, He said and hung up the phone.

(15)

The next day I went there in the doctor's car and waited for him at the entrance. I saw him and with him Rahasya.

I was shocked to see her in Australia. I was so happy, I ran towards him. Why didn't you tell you were bringing her too, I said.

I was so excited, I went and hugged her at the airport. she pushed me away, Slapped me, What the hell are you doing, She said.

I couldn't believe my eyes for what I saw. Krissh tried to console her and by that time one of the cops saw this and arrived.
They pulled me back, They took their side arms and started to point at me telling to put my hands on my back and lay down on the floor.

This is a misunderstanding sir, I said. I was so scared and started to sweat. You have the right to remain silent, Anything you say will be held in the court, He said. Krissh tried to convince the cops but they took me to their custody. Rahasya was hiding behind Krissh.

When I saw this, I was completely down. I was in the investigating room with the mirror on the wall. One of the senior officers approached me, Take out your passports, He said. Search him, He said to one of his colleagues. Why are you here in Australia, He asked me. Dear sir, I was transferred to work here from India and I work as a radiology HOD in Strickland Cres, I said.

The girl who cried for help is my girlfriend.This is really a misunderstanding, I said. Krissh spoke to the officer and then that senior officer apologized to me immediately and send us the back door.

I didn't speak to him or her, I just loaded their bags into the car and drove. I drove them to my room.

Throughout the journey, there was utter silence. She went to the balcony to watch the view. We were talking inside. Rahul, Please try to understand, He said.

What's going on here, Why she's catching hold of your hand? Why is she hiding behind you? She ditched me and started to love you right.

I don't know what more would have happened, Maybe you guys would have shared the same bed also, I said.

Krissh slapped me. How cheap you talk, All these days I watched your back, helped her and treated her like my sister, He said. The argument was heating up. Stop it, Rahul, this minute, He said.

Do you know anything about what happened in India? Don't talk like an idiot, He said.

The day you left Kochi and came back to Bangalore, I received a news, Rahasya met with an accident, I arranged for some people to look after her immediately rushing to the hospital.

After she got herself admitted, I sent you to Australia, I didn't want you to lose this wonderful opportunity. Remember that you were from a poor family, He said. I transferred her from Kochi and then she had undergone many tests.

Finally, the doctor said that she was in a coma. I tried my heart out to tell you, but I didn't want you to suffer in Australia or just abandon your post.

I tried my level best to bring out from the coma. The doctor said only happy thoughts would bring her back. And she came back normal after a month but then we came to know that her memories were lost.

I had also arranged for her parents to be in Bangalore. And she remembered only her parents. Somehow I gained her trust from few days, Introduced myself and how she's related to me.
I brought her here hoping she will remember you. I want you to win her again in your life, He said. I was shocked to hear all these I couldn't even speak anything. I looked at her.

I know how you are feeling right now, He said. We will work this out together. Trust me, You can do

this, He said. I sat there in the corner and cried
badly.

He called her inside. Well, Rahasya, This is Rahul,
He works in this hospital and designated as the head
of the department of radiology, He said. Nice to
meet you, Rahul, She said. Am sorry,

All of a sudden you came and hugged me. I didn't
know you, I didn't know what to do. But I'm very
sorry, She said.

It's okay Rahasya. What was your name again? She
said. I felt so bad to see her like this. My heart
broke. I couldn't bear the pain. My eyes were filled
with tears. Why are you crying, She said.

No, It's just dust in my eyes, I said. Rahasya, take a
shower and food will be ready, and after that take
rest, Krissh said.

Rahul, I want to know about nearby hotels. Am so
hungry and also I'll bring for Rahasya, He said.
Don't worry brother, I'll cook for all of us, I said.
Oh! You cook too huh? He said. Come on buddy,
You know am one of the greatest cooks in India, I
said.

Yeah, Greatest maggie maker of the world too, He
said with a silly laugh. Don't worry guys, I'll cook,
She said. Why do you need the stress dear, After all,
you are my guest,

So I'll cook, I said. Well, That's the kitchen, This is the living room, This is the bedroom, I was telling to Rahasya. Are there any dance studios here? She asked me. You don't even dance and why do you need a studio? I said. How do you know that? After all, I'm a good western dancer, She said.

I looked at Krissh's face. He was making faces nodding his head from side to side signaling me, Not to tell anything. Alright, Let me see what I can do for you, I said. Krissh pulled me into a corner.

Bro, Always act like you don't know her. Never tell anything about your past. She's into dance nowadays, So try to search a dance studio and she will do the rest, He said. But bro, She never used to dance, never cooks at all.

In that how did she learn all these, I said. I don't know, But after that accident, It became so weird that she started to cook, stated to dance, In fact, she even sings good, He said.

I was completely shocked to hear this.

Here's the towel, take a shower, I'll arrange for lunch by the time you get ready, I said. Thank you, She said with a beautiful tone.

I decided to gain trust with her first. I needed to start from first, I want myself to fall in love all over again and show her what's true love is, I said to myself.

I started to cook. I made rice first, I made radish sambar, It's one of the famous sambars in Karnataka, Along with that, I made papad for the side dish and also homemade mango pickle which was sent by my mother.

Krissh was helping me with the cooking. She was ready and she came into the living room. Where is the remote Rahul, She asked?

Just a minute, I'll help you with that, I said. I switched on the tv and then handed over the remote. Ammu, Here, there are no Indian channels, It's just Hollywood.

But one of my friends had told me that with tata sky dish it can broadcast all the Indian channels. Don't worry, I'll fix it soon, I said. Ammu? She asked and looked at my face with an embarrassment.

Sorry Rahasya, Your mother used to call that. How do you know my mother? She said. Krissh is a friend of mine, Your mother is well known for him, So like that, I know her, I said. I needed to lie, But am not good at lying, I thought to myself.

Every time I lied, It was a heartbreaking moment for me. I never lied to my Ammu. Arrange the table Krissh, I said. After arranging all the food on the dining table, I called Rahasya to have lunch. We sat together and had lunch.

There was complete silence in the dining room. I
could only hear the munching sound of the food.

We had a lot of eye contacts. After having lunch, I
washed all the dishes. Rahasya insisted to wash the
dishes, But I refused. And I went to buy some
groceries.

(16)

I knew a Dr in the hospital who recently became a good friend. He was a psychiatrist.
He's from India as well and his name was Dr.Nandan.
I spoke with him regarding Rahasya's issues. Well, Rahul, I want to meet her and speak with her in private.

Bring her over to my house this Saturday and you are on leave too. I'll deal with the rest, He said. I agreed to this.

After my work hours, I went home as usual. I want to speak with you Rahasya, It'll take a moment, I said. What is it? Krissh asked.
I have arranged a small meeting this Saturday with a doctor, He's a psychiatrist. I have told about Rahasya, So he wants to meet her and speak with her, I said. What? Why? She asked.

See Rahul, Am completely fine,
I don't have any trouble with my life so far.
Why are you forcing me to do things like this, That too without my permission how could you arrange a meeting with a doctor? She asked.

I'm sorry Rahasya, But there are things you don't remember, Please don't be angry, It's just a visit and he might help you bring some memories which are

lost, I said. I don't want to remember my past life,
Just leave me alone,

She said with anger and slammed the room door
and went inside crying. Krissh came and sat beside
me. What happened bro? I know you are trying
hard. I'll tell you something, After this meeting,
You better arrange a job for her here.
Let her stay with you. If you want, I'll go back to
India, He said. No, Don't go, Stay here, I said.
Okay, As you said, I'll arrange this job for her as a
nurse, Anyway, she has completed the course.
But Krissh, All her documents are in India, I said.
No bro, I have bought all the documents,
Don't worry about that, He said. Now go, Convince
her, He said. I went near the door and knocked. Go
away, She said.
I'm sorry Rahasya, Just open the door, I want to
speak with you, I said.
She opened the door. Her eyes were all red and hair
all over her face, What is it? She asked.
Okay, Come here, Sit down.
Ammu, there are so many things I want you to
remember, I know you very well,
I can tell everything about you perfectly, I said.
How do you know about me? She asked.
I'll tell you that later. Now get up, Wash your face
and don't be angry, I said. Okay, She said.

Hello dear Rahasya, I'm Dr. Nandan.
Nice to meet you.
Make yourself comfortable at home.
Namaste sir, She said.

Hello Rahul, Hello Krissh, He said.

Welcome, Sit down both of you, He said.

Chenamma, Bring something to eat for our guests, He said to his maid. Well, how is Australia Rahaysa? He asked.

It's awesome to be abroad sir, but it's hot.

Moreover, Rahul treats us like his family, She said.

That's nice of you Rahul. In fact, Rahul speaks more about you Rahasya, He said.

Rahasya gave me a big stare as if am the terrorist and plotting something against her family overnight.

Have some ice tea Krissh, He said.

After a few minutes, Rahul, I need you to go out and have some good time in the garden with krissh, Enjoy nature. In the meanwhile I need to speak with Rahasya in person, He said.

Sure doctor, Come Krissh. Rahasya, We will be out, Don't worry, I said.

After an hour, the doctor came out. Well, Rahul, I spoke with her, I even made an attempt at hypnotherapy.

I didn't see her speaking of you, She was continuously speaking of how she regrets the loss of her memories after the accident, She also feels pain for the people whom she cared and now they don't even exist in her mind.

She also asked me a question. The question was, Doctor, What if I had a boyfriend? What if I had fallen in love and I don't remember him?,

I convinced her from my side. Rahul, I can't give any guarantee for her memories,
It might return or she may be like this forever, He said. I need you to win her again, That's the only possible way, He said.

I sat there for a moment. Krissh came and convinced me. I went to Rahasya, So how do you feel Ammu? I said.
Am good Rahul, Actually, I want to speak with you in private, She said.
Krissh looked at my face. Alright, Where do you want to go? I said.
Take me somewhere alone, Maybe for a long drive, She said. Okay, Rahasya,
Today evening let's leave and drive away to the sunset, I said. What about me? Krissh said.
You stay at my house, I'll have some fun, I said. "Kalla," (*in Malayalam Kalla means robber*) Krissh said.

I paid the fees to the doctor, He refused, We are family, I don't accept fees from family, He said.

(17)

The same day evening, We drove. At first, It was the usual city and traffic.
All I could hear was horns and mobiles. Later as we passed the outskirts, I heard utter silence. I looked at her face through the rearview mirror, She was sitting peacefully, She loved the nature. What do you like to eat Rahasya? I said.

Nothing much, I'm not hungry, she said. No, I didn't mean right now, I wanted to know about your favorites, I said.

I don't think I do have a favorite, She said. Oh! come on, There should be something, I said.
Well, I do love ice creams, She said.

That's good. What about activities? I said.
I love dancing, singing, boxing, and art.
What is the most favorite of these? I asked?
Actually, One of my dreams is to learn sign language. I want to dance at the same time express the sign language so that the deaf people will come to know what am telling the world through dance.

That's wonderful Ammu, I said.
I thought for a second what a wonderful idea it is.
I drove to an ice cream parlor. Before I parked the vehicle, I want to ask you something Rahul, She said.
Well, we arrived at the Ice cream parlor.

Let's go and eat, I said.

I told I want to ask you something, She said.
Come Rahasya, Let's sit in the parlor and speak.
Nobody will disturb us, I said.
We walked in and I asked her what type of an ice cream does she want?

I'm happy with any ice cream Rahul, She said.
I just need to speak with you something, She said.
Alright, Come here. Sit down, Let's speak, I said.
What is it? tell me, I asked?

Why do you call me Ammu? She said.
I told you this, Your mother used to call you like that and I know her, So I started to call you like that, I said.
That's a lie, I need you to tell me the truth, She said.
One thing I don't like about humans is lying. Please don't lie, She said.

Tell me how do you know me, She said.
Come on Ammu, I know you through Krissh.

He's a very good friend of you, I said. Okay, She said. I went to the counter, Ordered one for me.
Which one do you want? I asked?
DBC (*Death By Chocolate*) She said.
We will serve you by 10 minutes, Please take your seat sir, said the staff.

I went and sat opposite to Rahasya. She stared at me. I touched her hand, She moved her hand away from me. What is it? She asked?
It was such an embarrassing moment for me.
Nothing Rahasya, I said.
The waiter came and served the ice creams. I paid him a tip and he was happy about it.

When I was having ice cream I received a call.
It was Isabelle. I attended the call.
What's up Isabelle? How are you? I asked?
I'm fine Rahul, It's been a long time so I called you, She said.
Well, there's a news for you Isabelle, I said. What is it? She asked?
Rahasya is here with me. She came a week ago, Sorry I couldn't inform you, I said.
So you are enjoying with your wife, She said. No, Isabelle, I want to speak with you regarding this, Can I meet you up? I asked?
Sure, Why not? She said. Well, Am coming right now with Rahasya, I said.

I hung up the phone and texted her, When we are there, please don't tell her anything about love or don't ask her anything regarding me, Shes's just like a friend for now. I'll explain everything once I get there.

I received a reply with an okay and a question mark.

We got there.

(18)

Isabelle came near the car and hugged me saying, after a long time buddy.
She then went near Rahasya and hugged her too. I introduced Rahasya to Isabelle. Come in Rahasya, She said.

She offered us soft drinks. Krissh called me, My phone was in charge in Isabelle's room. Isabelle went and answered the phone.

Yes, This is Isabelle, She said.
He hung up the phone and called Rahasya.
Where are you, He said.

Wait, I'll give the phone to Rahul, She said.
I spoke to him. Bro, Where is your phone? He said.
Don't worry, The person who answered my phone is an old friend, I said.
I want to meet that young lady, He said. Of course bro, I'll be back by night, I said.
No, You gotta stay here and spend the rest of the night, Isabelle said.
Okay, Krissh, Let me see, I'll let you know, I said.
Is there one more room for another person? I said to Isabelle.
Of course, Rahul, She said. Are you sure? I asked?
Yeah! Rahul, After all, He's family. Call him, She said.

I called Krissh. Buddy, I need you to take a cab and then hand him over the phone, I'll speak to him, I said.

Why brother, What happened He asked?

You are gonna come here and spend the rest of the night with us, and also you said something about meeting her. So get ready, I said.

I'm coming immediately, He said. He did as I said and he arrived at the house.

Hello Krissh, How are you? Isabelle asked?

Krissh stood like a statue carved out of stone and started to stare at her with eyes wide open.

He was looking though as if he was high on weeds.

Krissh, I said loudly. Sorry, Nice to meet you Ms? he said. Isabelle, She said.

Nice to meet you too Mr. Krissh, You have a unique name, She said.

He gave a silly laugh.

Do you live alone Isabelle? He asked?

Yeah! Krissh, She said. Are you engaged in a relationship, He said. Isabelle looked at me and smiled, Why do you ask such a question She asked?

Nothing, Just like that, He said.

After that, we spent outside on the porch having tea and talking stuff. Well, I'll start to cook us for dinner, She said.

I looked at Krissh, He winked at me.

I never understood why he winked at me. I'll help you, I said. No, I don't want any help from you guys, today you all are my guest, so I'll prepare, She said.

I sat with Rahasya and started speaking to her. Krissh ran behind Isabelle to the kitchen.

Hello Isabelle, If you need a hand? then I'm there, Krissh said.

No, Krissh, You sit down with Rahul and Rahasya. I'll prepare, She said. Oh, Come on Isabelle, I'd love to help you, He said.
Well, If you insist then sure, you can join me, She said.
He started to help her in the kitchen.

I don't know what got into him.

By 7:30 pm dinner was ready. I helped Isabelle to arrange the table. I sat with Rahasya, He sat beside Isabelle. Isabelle gave a look at me and then she showed towards him and she raised her eyebrows.

That expression meant what's with him? I shook my head intimating nothing.
We had dinner. It was tasty She served bacon and sausage with some vegetables and chips.

Krissh knew very well about the Australian dinner and these things never fill our stomach, So while he came from the room he bought a kg of rice and that was suitable for the sausage.

Krissh made rice and he served that. He made chicken too. He asked Isabelle to give a try. As it was her first time, She refused.

But still, Krissh forced her and she finally had. It is really tasty, She said.
That's Indian food, He said.
So we had our dinner. Isabelle, After cleaning let's go for a walk, He said.

I was looking at Krissh and he winked at me.
Sure Krissh, she said.
Rahul, Bring Rahasya with us, She said. Krissh put his hand on his forehead and gave me a disgusting look.

We all went for a walk. I was with Isabelle and Rahasya was with Krissh.
Krissh came to me. Go to your future wife idiot, he whispered.
As I came forward, He walked with Isabelle. As we were walking Rahasya said, Rahul, Doesn't it seem a bit awkward me walking with you and Krissh walking with Isabelle.

Why did you feel like that? I asked.
No, I didn't mean like that Krissh.

It's that Krissh and Isabelle are a good pair. They can get married right, She said.
So what about us? I asked.
What about us? She asked me.
Ah! nothing dear, I said.

Krissh was speaking with Isabelle Regarding a job for Rahasya.
Well, I know someone who can give her a job, Isabelle said.
Then It would be wonderful, I said. Rahasya too was excited working with the Australians.

Rahasya, Give me all your documents and I'll see that you get a job soon, She said.

It was time to sleep, Krissh sat on the chair which was on the porch outside, Rahasya was with Isabelle.
I myself went to speak with Krissh.

He was enjoying the breeze. Aren't you going to sleep? I said.
Nah! I've been thinking about Isabelle, bro, he said.
What about her? I said.

She's beautiful, lonely, beautiful, he said.
You repeated that already, I said.
I think am in love brother, he said.
I laughed loudly.
Come on bro, It's time, Let's sleep, I said.

The next morning Isabelle woke up and she went for a walk, I woke up and Krissh too, Go with her for a walk, I'm a bit tired, I'll sleep, I said.
I'll go, he said. Actually, I wasn't sleepy.
I wanted to follow these guys to check what will Krissh speak.
He helped her with milk as the milk van arrived.

Isabelle, Can I speak to you now? he said.
Of course Krissh, What's the matter? she said.
Let's walk then we will speak.

Here Rahul and Rahasya are sleeping so I don't want to disturb, he said. Yeah! let's walk, she said.
As they were walking they entered a road which was covered with trees.
It was a lonely road. It's awesome to hear these birds chirp, she said.
Every morning I come here, I hear them singing so beautifully. God has created each one for a reason. Especially human beings. We face a lot of problems every day and some problems and situations are beyond the limitations but still, there will be a solution, That's how the god plays, she said.

Don't think am mad, telling you all these kinds of stuff. I loved a guy so sincerely.
As soon as this was told I saw Krissh's face. He was in pain.

At first, Even he treated me with love and care and never left me alone. As the days went he started to avoid me, I loved him for one and a half year. He stopped replying to my messages, he stopped calling me, he stopped coming to see me, even though he knew am an orphan, he stopped caring me.

One day he answered my call and I said I want to meet him. He came to meet me, Why aren't you

replying my calls, emails or messages? Why are you avoiding me? I asked him?
I'm in love with another girl, he said.
I just loved you for time sake, It's over between us, he said.

I broked my heart and started to cry Krissh.
I was totally broken. He just left me in the middle of the road and went away.

Krissh was sad and eventually, he cried. I'm sorry to hear this Isabelle, he said.
By the way, you wanted to tell me something. What was it? she said.
Nothing Isabelle, It's nothing he said.

They walked further and climbed a hill and sat at the viewpoint of a beautiful scenery. Krissh said, Isabelle, What if I join with you and let's take revenge on him?

I mean not a revenge. It's that let's teach a lesson, He said. I don't want him to suffer Krissh,
After all, he's with somebody else.
So let him be happy, she said.
Come on Isabelle, Don't worry. My intention is not to hurt him but will teach a lesson so that he won't repeat the mistake with her, He said.

Well, hmmm, okay, she said. Now, what if he returns to you and asks for forgiveness and he wants to get back to you, Are you ready to give another chance to him he asked?

Definitely, I'll give him another chance, she said.
Well, Starting from today let's start the game, he
said. Oh, Krissh! she said and laughed at him.
I returned home as they were coming back.

Where were you? Rahasya asked.
I just went for a walk, I said.
Where are others? she asked.
They might be here somewhere, Ah! here they
come, I said.
Where were you, people? I was worried, she said.
Chill, we just went for a walk, Morning air is fresh
here in the countryside, Isabelle said.

Alright get ready, let's make some breakfast, she
said.
I went outside and sat under a tree. Rahasya saw me
and came.
What are you doing Rahul? she asked.
Just taking the fresh air, come, sit down here, I said.
Well, Are you ready to join for a job here? I asked.
Yeah! I should get used to it Rahul, After all, It's
Australia, she said.
Oh! you love birds, Will you please come to have
coffee, Isabelle shouted.
I looked at her face and she made an eye contact
and smiled with shy.
Well, come, let's have, I said.

Krissh, I need you to arrange every document of
Rahasya and then meet me at this hospital, Ask her
to wear something western, like formals.

I'll handle the rest, Isabelle said. Okay, Isabelle, Krissh said.

(19)

The next day I went to work, I trusted Isabelle so I know she will take care of things. Rahasya went with Krissh to attend the interview.
After a few minutes, I got a call. I answered it. Rahasya was on the line. Rahul, yes Rahasya. I got the job as a nurse here, Am so happy.

Thank you Krissh, I love you, she said.
Am sorry? I said. Oh! sorry, Krissh, I didn't mean like that, she said.
It's okay ma, I was kidding, I said.
I was so happy, I bought sweets and distributed in my workplace.

That evening I went to my room with a cake and two bottles of wine.
I invited Isabelle.
She was home soon and Krissh with Rahasya too.

I was late, I came home and saw them waiting for me. As soon as I saw I screamed "surprise."
By their looks, I felt like they already knew the plan.

After that, I arranged the cake on the table and wine bottles too.
The cake was a black forest mixed with berries and on top, it was written: "Congratulations Rahasya, All the best".

Rahasya blew the candle and we all applauded.
Let's drink, Krissh said. Are you ready to drink Isabelle asked?
I was born ready, Krissh said. Do you drink Krissh? Isabelle asked?
Well, I drink only wine and breezer, except that I won't touch alcohol, Krissh said.

Oh! I thought wine was made up of milk, Isabelle said. Rahasya laughed out loud, Isabelle had a smile on her face.
She started to tease Krissh. Come on, Isabelle, I don't drink actually.
But in Kerala, we will have this grape wine, It's homemade, Krissh said.
I was kidding dear, chill out, said Isabelle.
We all drank the wine and then enjoyed the day.

I wanted to ask you this from so many days, said Rahasya. Tell me, What is it asked Krissh?

The day I came here, I noticed a door which is locked. It's not been open. I just wanted to see what is inside Krissh, said Rahasya.

It's just a storeroom, I interfered. Okay, Well It's locked.
I can clean it and use it for some other purpose, Rahasya said.
No, the key is been lost, It's okay, Leave it, I said.

Rahasya felt something was wrong with what I said.
I came to know that through her expressions.

<u>ACT 5: The Revenge of Isabelle</u>

(20)

What's his name Isabelle? I asked, sitting on the balcony with a cup of coffee.
Krissh was sitting with me. His name is Hawkings.

Is it his first name or? I gave a pause.
No, his first name is William, William Hawkings.
That's a wonderful name, Krissh said.
I stared at Krissh. Sorry, I didn't mean like that, Krissh said.

It's okay Krissh, let him do whatever he wants, in fact, I don't even mind him now, she said.
Oh come on, Where does he stay Krissh asked?

He stays a couple of blocks from here in an apartment, she said.
Alright then, Let's teach him some lesson, he said.
Where does he usually go? Krissh asked?
He sits in the Kingston. It's a pub or a bar, she said.
Well, what are we waiting for? Let's go, Krissh said.

I myself as the in charge of the radiology department, I got some advantages. All I need to do is that the work should go in a smooth flow. I made some calls and went with Isabelle and Krissh.

Isabelle had an old friend who lived in the city. Her name was Loveline. She gave us 3 bi-cycles. It's fun to ride a bicycle in the city. After all, no traffic, no tensions.
Due to tall buildings and skyscrapers no much heat too.

We rode together and finally reached the Kingston. Before entering, you catch hold of my hand, Krissh said.
I didn't get you, she said. Just hold my hand like in the Hollywood movies the couples walk to the dance floor, Krissh said.

Oh! I understood, she said.
She put her arms inside Krissh's arms, They looked like a perfect pair.
They walked inside followed by me in the back.
As soon as they entered, she whispered, he's sitting over there and talking with that girl.

He looked tall and fair, his eyes were blue, physically athletic fit and he was kind of a romantic to see.
Any kind of girl would fall for him.
He wore a Rolex watch and his boots were made of fine quality of leather. He was rich and he looked decent and funky. A mixture of both I'd say.

Krissh went aside and pulled out a chair for Isabelle. My lady, please sit down while I order, before that select what you want, he said.

Krissh sat with her and I sat facing Krissh and Isabelle.

These were noticed by William. Krissh's behavior was so gentle. It was exactly like seeing a movie in real.

Krissh, How do you act so well? she asked.
Well, I do watch a lot of Hollywood movies Isabelle, he said.
I laughed. Don't laugh like that, Rahul, maintain the act. Let him feel the pain, he said.
Alright, don't worry, I said.

Suddenly, he stood up from that place and walked towards us.
As he came, Isabelle held Krissh's hand so tight.
Maybe she was scared of him.

Hello there, Isabelle. How are you? he said. Am fine.
Well, Who are these idiots you are hanging with? he asked.
Krissh doesn't like speaking without respect.

Immediately he yelled, Excuse me? Who is the big ass with a small dick who's standing in front of me and calling us an ass?
The whole restaurant heard that and some were murmuring regarding his small dick.
He was offended. I'll take care of you later, William said.

Oh, come on! I have seen a lot of dicks like you.
You touch me, I'll bring the whole army, he said.
Isabelle stood up and pushed him away. Why are you behaving like an ass?

And for your kind information, they are not idiots, they are well-educated people who have a heart and they are from India, she said.
The restaurant security came. What's the matter, madame with a French accent he asked?

Nothing sir, This person was just leaving, she said referring to William.
He put his head down in shame and drove away.
Damn! His car was a Ferrari 488 GTB, I thought to myself.

That was completely poor handling, I said to myself.
It's okay, Krissh said.

Isabelle started to cry. Why are you crying, Isabelle I asked?
I never scolded him like that in my entire life, she said.
Now stop crying Isabelle, I said.

Isabelle, This will often happen from now on, he said.
You should be strong.
That day I decided to take Rahasya to the same restaurant. Hey guys, tonight let's come here to have dinner, All of us, I said.

Sure, That's a good idea, Krissh said.
He will be here in the restaurant, she said.
That's good. When there is a girl there won't be any issues, I said.

Come on, How do I look, Isabelle asked?
You look like a queen, Krissh said.

That same night, I came with Rahasya and Krissh with Isabelle.
William was playing snooker and there was a jukebox where music was playing.
It was the classics.
As Krissh entered he stared at him. I said the whole incident to Rahasya so she was maintaining the distance and was prepared.

Krissh ordered. We started to eat. Krissh was so romantic with Isabelle.
Is he in love with Isabelle Rahasya asked?
I nodded my head saying yes.

Did he propose to her she asked?
I nodded my head saying no. He loves her but she loves William, so he decided to patch up her with William, a sacrifice, I said.

Rahasya opened her eyes and mouth wide. She was surprised.
What happened? I asked.
No, Am actually wondering that even in this generation there are people who sacrifice their love just for others, she said.

Well, yeah! this is your live example, I said.

Can I ask you something? she said.
Yeah of course, What is it? I said.
Did I have a boyfriend before my accident and then
did I forget that person due to memory loss, she
asked?

I was speechless and at the time.
William interfered. Isabelle, I want to speak with
you.
She stood up, William, this is a restaurant and I
don't want any kind of scenario to happen here, she
said.

It's nothing, I just want to speak with you, he said.
Well, Am not interested. There are so many women
who are interested in you, go speak with them, she
said.

He started to shout, You sitting here with these
gringo's and how dare you to avoid me, he said.
Even though he looked good, he had no respect
towards the outsiders, especially Indians.
The most he hated was Indians.
Go away, I don't love you anymore, she said.
I just want to speak with you, he said. Krissh turned
towards her.

He's asking so much Isabelle, go dear, I said.
Please Krissh, Don't force me. I hate him so much,
He ditched me Krissh, she said.

Just go away, she said to him and he put his head
down and went away.

Krissh sat silently. What did Krissh do Isabelle? I
asked. Oh no! I didn't scold him, Rahul, I just
wanted to play along with Krissh, Isabelle said.
Am very sorry Krissh, she said.

It's okay dear, I thought you really scolded me,
Krissh said. Am sorry Krissh, I really didn't mean to
hurt you, I just went with the flow, she said.
It's okay Isabelle. Am okay now, Krissh said.
We had the dinner silently.

After dinner, Krissh said, Who is ready for dessert?
Rahasya looked at me, I raised my eyebrows, she
nodded her head referring to no.
Don't worry, this will be common from now on,
have something, I said to Rahasya.
Alright, You two lovebirds sit here, I'll go out with
Isabelle for a walk and will reach home.

You better take a cab back home, said Krissh.
I was scared that he might come back and make an
issue, so I planned to send back Rahasya in a cab
and follow Krissh.

I followed Krissh and he was walking silently with
Isabelle, she was looking down.
Isabelle, you know how much am trying for this,
don't worry.

She cried so badly, Krissh didn't know what to do. He took out a handkerchief and handed it over to her.

She hugged Krissh immediately and cried. He was shocked and he felt so bad for her.

At first, He didn't touch her, but then he slowly kept his hands on her hair and consoled her.

William was standing nearby. He saw the whole incident. He just walked towards them and he slapped Krissh.

I couldn't bear that, When I was about to go and stop this, Krissh hit him back.

Who the hell are you to hit me, William's asked?
Krissh held her hand.
I'm her soulmate, I'm her lover, I'm her husband, Now what will you do? Asked Krissh?

Hearing these words, Isabelle was surprised and she was speechless.
She didn't speak anything but looked at Krissh in amaze. When William raised his hand to hit him again, Stop it, she shouted loudly at William.

Isabelle, after all, am your lover, I loved you so much and you cheat me for him, he said. Did I ditch you? Did I give up you for him? she said angrily.

He put his head down. I gave an entry. I want to speak with you in person, I said to William.
Isabelle looked at me with so much anger, What do you want to speak with him, she asked?

Leave it, Isabelle, I'll take care of this, I said. I looked at Krissh and signaled for him to take her away. Let's go, Isabelle, he said.
William looked at me. What do you want to speak, he asked?
Let's go somewhere else, I said.
We both went to a lonely place.
It was a grazing field and a few coconut trees were there. William, I don't know anything about you, I don't know who are you, I don't know what do you do. All I know is your rich and you loved Isabelle and then later ditched her and went away.
She suffered a lot of pain and been without you for almost a year and then later Krissh fell in love with her and when he found out that still, she loves you, he decided to sacrifice his love for the both of you.

Love is not a game or some play time. It is a priceless feeling which only comes once in a life, I said.
William didn't answer anything.
He sat there for almost 30 minutes without a word. I sat there and waited for his answer.
I don't know what felt in him.

After 30 minutes.
Yes, I know I've been an asshole, I've slept with many girls, I'm a womanizer, I've been a shit all her life, I ditched her at last because I used her enough.
What I've been doing was wrong.
I understand that now, he said.

I need you to bring her to Kosciuszko national park.

Why, I asked?
Just bring her, and it's better to bring Krissh too, he said. Well, okay William, I said and went away.

(21)

The next day, I came along with Isabelle, Rahasya,
and Krissh, Isabelle was very curious,
I told Krissh about this before.
Even Krissh was very curious about his answer.

We reached the Kosciuszko national park. The park
is situated in new south wales near to Victorian
border, Its 216 km via Boboyan road.
It took us 3 hours to reach the destination. We went
by car, Krissh drove the car.

The national park is natures gift, It was so cold and
snowy all over the park.
The park is famous for its mountain Kosciuszko and
it's the highest peak in Australia hence the name
Kosciuszko national park.

It was so cold Isabelle and Rahasya hired a woolen
coat. We were waiting in burning log restaurant.
It's famous for beers and fast food. It is situated in
mount Tate road.

William's arrived, yes, how are you, Rahul? he
asked. Come on sit down, treat's mine, he said.
Isabelle looked at me in despair. Krissh was happy
and at the same time, he was sad thinking about
letting go of her.

Hello Isabelle, Willaim said.
First of all, I'm very sorry for behaving like shit.

Second, I'm very sorry for hitting Krissh, he said.

He hit you, Rahasya said in wonder.
She didn't know about this fight.
I looked at her and signaled her to be silent.
She tilted her head intimating okay.
Third, I need you to forgive me, he said.

Isabelle's eyes were filled with tears, but she controlled. Apology accepted, she said.
I need to tell you one another thing, he said.

Krissh's eyes opened wide, and Isabelle had a confused expression.
What is it? she asked.
I had loved you but misused you, I was a fool to ditch you for another woman.
I'm very sorry for all this. I realize the mistake I did.

I want you to be with Krissh, He's perfect for you, he said. Krissh stood up in wonder, Isabelle was speechless.
Her eyes were wide open.

Rahasya was dreaming and she took a long breath and lifted her shoulders a bit with eyes wide open.
I myself was looking straight into the eyes of William. I don't want you to say anything, just accept him, he said.

Krissh went out. He loves you more than anything, I can see this in his eyes, he will look after you like his own family, he said.

William's, You are such a lovely man, you have a good heart.

If this makes you happy then definitely I'll marry him, she said.

On the other hand, without my knowledge, I fell in love with him, she said.

Rahasya looked at me, I smiled at her. Let's go outside and speak with him, he said.

We all went outside and we saw there Krissh wiping his tears.

Your tears will freeze up man, I said.

He looked at me and started to smile.

Now, why are you crying? she asked.

Ah! nothing, Come on Krissh, Once upon a time there was a cute little bird who used to sit in a tree.

Then, I said.

Then eventually that little bird started to sing because that bird found his soul mate.

The end, she said.

Such a cute horror story, William's said. We all laughed and Krissh slowly cheered up.

By the way, who was that bird, Krissh asked?

You are a dumbo, Isabelle said.

One bird is me and another one is you, she said.

Krissh started to blush.

What about you and Rahasya? William's asked me.

Let's eat ice cream, Isabelle said and changed the topic.

Rahasya looked at me and then asked William, what about me and him?
By that time Krissh had already whispered about this. Nothing Rahasya, I was asking about the job, he said. Rahasya had a strong doubt about this.

Later, we all booked a big cable wire and enjoyed the mountain breeze on that. It was freezing but still, it was feeling good.

That evening we all went to our homes and William's bid goodbye as he was flying to Malaysia regarding a conference meeting.

(*That night Rahasya will have no sleep.*
She keeps walking, Sits on the balcony.)

I woke up in the middle of the night to drink water.
I see her having trouble with her sleep.
Even though there was a chair she used to sit down.

So I made tea and sat with her. What's the matter Ammu, I asked?
I really have a doubt, Rahul.
I want to know whether did I love somebody or not before my accident? It's been bugging me for a while, she said.

Well, forget that and come sleep. You think a lot and tomorrow you have work.

You should have proper sleep or it might affect your health, I said. And you are giving me tea, great, she said and laughed.

The next day she woke up. Krissh, I had a dream yesterday, she said.
What is it? he asked.
I saw a dream where Rahul was my lover, she said.
I started to sweat.
Chill Rahasya. Get ready and go to work, he said.

I need you to make a plan, I need you to make her remember, he said.
But what shall I do? I asked.
Try to recreate your love story, he said.
But brother, It's very hard here in Australia and moreover, if I do that, I may get a bad opinion, he said.
Okay let's see what we can do, he said.
That day I left one of my room unlocked and went to work.

Rahasya arrived early, She had been into that room. I reached home from work as usual. As soon as I came, she went inside her room.
I was not sure what happened. She came out with one of our photo in Kochi and started to cry. Where did you find that? I asked.
She opened that door.
See, you have locked the door saying it was a store room and this is what I see? She said.
The room was arranged with every moment I spent with her, each and every photo were framed and

kept inside. Each and every used item by Rahasya was kept inside that room, her slippers, her small sized clothes, bouquet, tissues, bangles, rings, empty perfume bottles, etc.

Everything was kept inside. Seeing this she started to cry. Why did you hide this from me, she said?
Why did you lie to me, she said?
I had no words, I started to cry slowly. Her tears slowly rolled down her cheeks.
Even Krissh didn't know about this. She ran to her room and slammed the door.

Krissh stood in surprise and was speechless. He didn't know what to tell. I sat down on diwaan and started to think everything about our past. Krissh came and sat beside me.

Why didn't you tell me about this Rahul, he asked?
It's that........ I paused. Alright, now leave it, he said.
Come on, get your ass up and convince her, he said.
What shall I tell her, I asked?
Don't worry about that, just go there and then you will get that flow, he said.
I went towards the room, I knocked on the door.
She opened, Am sorry I said.

Her eyes were swollen like a ripe pumpkin. Please don't cry, I know what I did is wrong, but tell me anything, I'll do it for you, I said.
She didn't speak anything. She locked herself in her room until dinner time.

She had her dinner and stopped even looking at my
face. I tried to speak to her but she didn't respond to
anything. She just went ahead as if I don't exist.

(22)

Next morning, she woke up and got ready and told Krissh that she's leaving to work.
I heard her voice, so I went to see her. So soon huh? I said.
She didn't speak anything. She just closed the door and went away.
It was heartbroken for me. I couldn't do anything rather than see her leave.

"Whatever happens, It happens for good", Krissh said. He said as the supreme Vishnu came in the avatar of Krishna.

I was pissed off. Come on buddy. Don't be angry, One day you will thank me, he said.
I went to shower and went to work as usual.
I was sitting in my cabin supporting my head on a wall and was watching out through the window.

It was raining badly, the news announced that some huge Hurricane was passing through the oceans of the Pacific in the east around the Tasmanian sea.
The storm was huge enough to uproot trees and throw away huge trucks.
The military announced us to stay inside. Even in that storm, my heartbreak was the most painful one.
I called Rahasya's phone, but she never answered.

I tried calling her 20 to 30 times. the 30th time she answered my call. I'm very busy, Due to storm patients have become more. Paperworks are piling up, Ms. Kathy, could you please help me, she said.

For a moment there I thought she was telling to me. I started to smile and I kept telling repeatedly hmmm, hmmm.

After some time, please stop calling me, she said in an angry voice. hmmm, I said and before I said that, she hung up.

I felt like am the stupidest guy in the world.

So many people lost the lives in this Hurricane, The flood washed out everything, there were so many money, documents, dead bodies all over the city.

It was the worst storm I had ever seen in my life, of course, even India has a storm but It was not like this.

The military was helping homeless people and they were supplying food and water, They were helping to find their missing ones including animals.

After my work I came out, It was still raining.

I didn't carry an umbrella. I walked back to the room like a hero walks into the Indian movie after a break up in the rain.

I was all drenched up. I was expecting her to come and scold me for getting wet in rain.

I knocked on the door. What is this? Why did you get wet in this rain, Krissh asked?

Nothing Krissh, I said and went to my room. I thought she was there, but it seemed like she didn't even come home.

Where is she, I asked Krissh? She didn't arrive yet, he said.

I was worried as the weather condition was horrible, so many thoughts passed.

I took the company car and drove to her office. It was so windy that my car started to push across the road. Somehow I reached. I saw her waiting inside the reception. She saw me but she pretended that she didn't see me. One of the receptionist is my friend. She pointed out me and said that I'm waiting for her.

Rahasya saw me in disappointment. Then she packed up her things and came. She sat in the back. I felt like am the driver who came to pick her up. I drove without saying a word.

After a few minutes, pullover, she said.

She came and sat in the front. You could have sat in the back, I said.

Drive, she said.

While driving, I got to change the gear. As I changed the gear, I touched her hand.

She looked at me like *Nagavalli, (It's a south Indian Kannada horror movie.)*

I thought maybe if I take her to an ice cream parlor then she might talk to me. But due to storm nothing was open except hospitals. I decided to make Pizza at home.

I reached home and was parking the car. I saw her running up. I parked the car and tried the lift, electricity was out. I decided to walk upstairs.

I went up and I saw her waiting up half the stairs near the window and watching out.

I coughed and she saw me.

She then walked upstairs with me. I opened the door with my spare key.

She went inside followed by me. Krissh was in the bathroom. He came out after some time. Hey, Hello people.

How's the storm today, he asked? I didn't answer, neither did she.

Come on, what's wrong with you people? Rahasya, come here, he said.

What is it? she said. Come, sit beside me. I want to speak to you.

She sat beside her.

Rahasya, now why are you angry with him, he asked?

You really don't know why I'm angry with him, she asked?

okay okay, he said. At least give him one chance da, he said.

She didn't speak anything but got up from her place and went to her room. I looked at Krissh.

Chill buddy, everything will turn out good, he said.

Krissh, she called. Bro, I need a dance class here, could you please find one, she asked?

alright, she said.

A few minutes later, Krissh approached me.

Buddy, can you do me a favor, he asked?

It's a dance class, right?

Well, yeah, he said. Thank you, bro.
And I'm going with Isabelle, he said.
In this storm?
Well, I felt like seeing her, he said.
Don't go Krissh, It's not the right time now, I said.
Okay, well, I'll call her, he said.

Isabelle called me, she was worried about me.
Krissh has told me everything, she said.
Rahul, don't worry. Everything will be alright, trust me, she said.
I'll come and stay with you for a few days if you don't mind, she said.
no problem Isabelle. You are always welcome to my home, I said.
In the middle of this, I had so many plans. I wanted to visit India, meet my parents, get them something.
I found out one dance class there.
It was called as Salsabor dance studio.
It had one of the highest ratings all over the city.
It was approximately 8km from home.
I spoke with the studio about her enrollment. I informed Krissh too.

She went to the studio and got herself enrolled. She spoke with her manager and started to go early to the office and by evening she used to go dancing.

Somehow in between a year passed. Still, we didn't speak. I didn't know exactly what was the mistake.
I didn't know where it went wrong.

(23)

After a year, as the part of my holidays, the company booked a ticket back home. Of course, It was just one and a half month. I informed Krissh too.

I packed all my clothes and bought some things for parents.
I bought some chocolates. My mother loves them.
Everything was packed and ready to go.
Krissh took the company car and drove me to the airport and Isabelle too was with him. Rahasya didn't come. She was at work.

I told Krissh not to inform her until she asks you.
We were at the airport and the flight was 30 minutes delayed.
Krissh, take care of her.
You know I will, he said. Isabelle, Please keep an eye on her, I said.
Krissh, just go safe and be back. Convey my greetings to your parents, she said.
I'll call you every day, I said to Krissh. Don't forget to lock the doors.
And Krissh, please don't mess it up, I said. He laughed out loud.
We hugged each other at the airport. Isabelle's eyes were filled with tears. Oh come on, He's not leaving forever, Krissh said.
I know Krissh, she said. Isabelle hugged me too.

I went past the security gate and then in the elevator
until they just disappeared from the view.

ACT 6: back to home town

(24)

I reached Trivandrum international airport. A friend of mine stays in Trivandrum. So, I borrowed his car to go to Pathanamthitta. I reached home by midnight at 01:30. All were sleeping. I parked my car and went ahead to the house.

I knocked on the door. Amma woke up and opened. As soon as she saw me, she hugged me and cried.
Tears were just all over my shirt. She was so happy to see me.
Father woke up seeing all these.
He never spoke to me and after so many years he started to speak to me.

I don't know what changed him. He was an alcoholic and I didn't see any drinks or empty bottles lying around.
My brother woke up and he smiled at me. I was confused for a minute.

What is he doing amma, I asked?
He's going to an IT company in town, He's earning around 12 thousand for a month, amma said. That's good, I said.

Appa got up and asked about my dinner. I still didn't have appa, I said. He asked amma to serve me and I had dinner.

It was the first time in months having dinner made by mom. The taste lifted my spirits.

After that, I drank the same old black tea. It's so awesome to drink black tea sitting in the canopy areas of my native, especially during winters. It feels like Coorg. I kept my bag aside in my room and slept, It was 02:30.

Next morning I woke up with a hot cup of black tea and then unpacked all my stuff. I gave the chocolates, perfume, clothes, tea powder, juice powder etc for my mom.

I had bought a watch for my father too. All these were purchased in the Australian airport. My father, with excitement, started to tell Oh! it's an Australian watch. He was happy.

I bought an iPhone for my brother, He was happy enough.
Later that evening around 4:00 I took mom to Malabar jewelers and asked her to select a gold chain for her.
She was so happy and surprised.

After 1 and a half hour in the jewelry, she finally selected a necklace and I bought that. In the meantime, I asked the father to select a ring and a bracelet.
He selected and I packed that too. They were so happy. I made a call to Krissh.

I reached Buddy, I said.
Everything's good here. She didn't ask about you, he said.
It's okay, anyway take care Krissh, I said and hung up the phone.

Appa, what is the amount of money you need to clear the debt, I asked.
Why Rahul?
Tell me, It's okay, I said.
40,000/-Rs balance is there, he said.
You had kept this debt and yet you didn't tell me. I would have paid this long time ago
Alright, Tell me who it is and I'll pay it, I said.

It's okay, Leave it, he said.
appa, Tell me, It's okay. I'm your son, I said.
Then he showed me their house and I paid the debt.

In the night after dinner, we sat in the verandah for some air. Appa was talking something about the relative's marriage. He also said me to join the marriage with him and mom.
Sure, I'll go with you guys, I said.

(25)

The next morning, We went to Marriage, The whole family kingdom had come there. All were dressed up so beautifully.
My mother's brother came towards me running and hugged me.

so soon grown up like a king, she said. I just smiled at him.
He's in Australia now, he's working there, amma said.
That's good. well, people are growing up soon and getting married, she said.
Well, time just flies, she said.

Mom then went ahead to talk with all the relatives, after all, it's a family wedding.
As I was sitting among the people, I caught a girl staring at me. She's the daughter of my aunty.
Her name is Atmika.
I raised my eyebrows and asked how are you?

I'm fine, just the heat, she said. She came and sat next to me. As we were talking, I caught her mother's attention.

She was watching and smiling. We were childhood friends, but then later somehow we got separated due to hard living.

Her mother went to my mother and started to talk.
They spoke something and looked at us and smiled
together. Then we sat for lunch together.
I heard amma telling you are in Australia, Is it true,
she asked?

Do you want to hear the truth or lie, I asked?
Tell me the lie, she said.
I'm still in Pathanamthitta, I said.
She laughed out loud. Well, this indicates that you
are in Australia, Right? she said.
Yeah! I said.

How's the living there, and the weather, she asked?
It's good Atmika, I said.

As the conversation went on, Atmika's mother
came. Mutthe, we are going today to Rahul's house,
she said.
Come on aunty, Your always welcome, I said.

We got up and then went to the marriage, took
photos and then I brought them in my car.
Is this your car, Aunty asked?
No aunty, It's one of my friend's car, I just borrowed
from him for a few days, I'll be going back to
Australia, I came here for my leave, I said.

When are you going back, Atmika asked?
I'll be going next month end, I said.
We reached home.

We were all sitting inside. Her mother wanted to speak something regarding a marriage.

Well, Kamakshi, I wanted to talk about my daughter's marriage, she said.
Wow, My baby girl is getting married, amma said.
Her father was sitting silently because everywhere these ladies are the loudspeakers.

No Kamakshi, I wanted to speak about my girl and your son, she said.
I looked at her and she was shocked to hear this. Of course, I was in shock, but I knew something was fishy.

Amma was ready for marriage. She immediately accepted. I looked at amma and appa and they knew something was wrong.
Aunty, I like your daughter, but I don't want to get married, I said.
When you like her then what's the problem, she asked? It's that, I paused.
Alright, Leave now, take her with you and go somewhere else, amma said.
I looked at her and smiled. Let's go, I said. She tilted her head.

We went in the car to nearby ice cream parlor.
What do you want, I asked?
Whatever you want, I'll eat that, she said.
I ordered the Royal park for us. It was so big that two people can eat in one.

After a few minutes, She started to speak.
Do you have any girlfriends?
Hmmm, I uttered.

What do you mean by hmmm, Is it girl space friends or girlfriend?
I'm in love with a girl called Rahasya and told all the stories about her.
She respected my privacy and didn't ask for anything much more than what I said.
I'm sorry Atmika, I can't marry you.
After all, You know the situation, I said.
Don't worry Rahul, I'll take care about this, she said.

After that, I went home.
Well, Dear Rahul, you are getting married to Atmika, Amma said.
Atmika stood in the middle of our family and said loudly, Aunty, Uncle, I very much like Rahul, but I don't have the intention to marry him, she said.
It's that we are very good friends, and I would love to stay like that forever, she said.

All were shocked to hear this. Her mother shouted at her. She shouted back, Stop it amma. All these years I have always listened to you.
At least regarding this, you should give me a chance, she said. Her mother became silent.

Suddenly I got a call from Krissh. I answered the call.
Buddy, It's been three days, These two days she was silent thinking you went to meet Isabelle.

But she's worried about you and started to ask me where you went, I said the truth that you left the country and went to India.
She thought you went forever. You may get a call from her, he said.
As I was standing among the family, I was just telling hmm…. hmm….
What happened buddy, Any problem, he asked?
Nothing Krissh, I'll hang up now, Take care, I said.
Who is it, Amma asked?
It's work ma, don't worry, I said.

Her mother was angry. I could see that from her face, Later appa spoke.
See Kamakshi, Both of them are very good friends.
If they don't like this then why to force them.

Their happiness is our happiness right, he said.
Everybody calmed down, and all sat down for dinner.
I myself didn't feel hungry, so I walked down the house near the trees.

I got a call from Krissh.
Yes, tell me, buddy, I said
There was no answer,
Hello, Krissh, are you able to hear me, I asked?
It's me, Rahasya said.
For a second I was speechless.
Tell me Rahasya, What's the matter, I asked?
How dare you leave me here, she said and started to cry.

As she spoke I could hear her voice getting cracked.
You didn't speak to me, so I thought you don't care,
I said.
I never told you that I don't care.
All of a sudden when I see my pictures with you,
how can I take it, how can I tolerate that you lied to
me, she said. I don't feel anything towards you all of
a sudden, I really need time, she said.
Alright, now leave that, Don't worry. Do you need
anything from my home, I asked.
nothing, she said.
Well, okay Ammu, I gotta go, have some work
here, I said and hung up.

Atmika came. Why are you sitting here in dark, she
asked?
Nothing ma, Just enjoying the air, I said.
Oh come on, I know about you, something's
bugging you, she said.
She just called me ma, I spoke to her. so kind of
disturbed that's all, I said.

Alright, come to have dinner. Please don't tell no, I
know you will tell no, but please, at least for me,
she said.
Alright come, I said.
Later that night she took selfies.

Almost 4 to 5 selfies were there. She uploaded on
her facebook and tagged me. That was later seen by
Rahasya. Krissh sent me a message. " brother, she's
totally burned by seeing your selfies with one girl."
She's completely gone mad over here, he said.

I didn't reply back. I had plans here in my place.

The next day I woke up and spoke with appa.
Appa, what is the cost of land here? any ideas, I said.
Here 1 cent is 2.5 lakhs rupees, he said. why Rahul, he asked?

Nothing appa, I wanted to own a land and construct a house for you guys, I said.
Can we go see the land, I asked him?
Sure, let's go tomorrow.

By the way, even we have some land, he said.
I didn't know about this. Okay well, I'll construct a house there only, but first, I need to see the land, I said.
Okay, no problem let's go now, he said.
I, Atmika and appa went to see the land. It was almost a km from our home. We reached there. This is big, Atmika said. How many cents are there, I asked appa?
It's almost 11 cents, he said. That's big enough for me to construct a palace, I said.
Palace? now that's what I call hard work, Atmika said.

(26)

Later that day I went to the construction developers
and properties called Ram builders. I went into their
office and spoke to the CEO.
Namaskaram sir, please have a seat.
Tea, coffee or cool drinks, he asked me?
Cool drinks might be good, I said.
I'm Shivan, how may I help you, he asked?
Namaskaram sir, I'm Rahul. I came here regarding a
civil engineer as am planning to construct a house
in my land, I said.

Of course, What about the documents, he asked me?
Everything is okay regarding the papers, I said.
Okay, Rahul, before we start I want to see the land
and we will start with the plan soon, he said.
We had a deal and then we shook hands and I came
back home.

Appa, I have spoken with the contractor. We will be
starting soon, I said.
Okay, Rahul, you know, am so happy that my son is
changed, he said.
Appa, am happy that you have changed, our family
is going to be noticed by our family, he said.
This is just the start, I have more plans, I said.
Rahul, I wish soon that house is constructed and I
need to come to your housewarming ceremony,
Atmika said.
I smiled at her.

Amma called us for dinner and we sat down together.
Atmika left the next day with her parents, I bid goodbye.

The next day I visited the bank and was done with every formality with the help of the bank manager. He was a lovely guy. I mailed to my company for a letter from HR to be shown to the bank so that it helps with the loan formality.

Finally, the loan was sanctioned and I went to the office and soon a contractor was appointed to me. His name was Ramdas.
He helped me with all the graph and plans. He also suggested some ideas with the help of his team.

Everything was done perfectly. Soon we went to a poojari. He fixed a good time and we started the Bhoomi Pooja. Finally the next day we started the construction. It was the happiest moment for me.
I didn't tell or invite anybody for the pooja.

Half a month got over, the construction was already started. I told appa to take care of the construction while I'll be gone back to work.

Appa, I'll take care of things from there. All I need is your eyes on the work, I said.
Don't worry Rahul, I'll take care with all my heart, he said.

Everything was going according to plan. Molding was done. And it was time for me to get back to Australia.
I bid farewell for family, Everything was arranged neatly. Ammu loves mango cut pickle, specially made in the home.

So I asked amma and said It's for me. So she prepared a box for me. Amma hugged and cried and appa's eyes filled with tears. I gave them some money before coming and I gave my brother some money and told him to spend it wisely. I drove the car back to Trivandrum.

I gave the car back with the tank filled up. He was happy, I went to the airport and boarded my flight.

ACT 7: back to work (Australia)

(27)

I landed and Krissh came to pick up. I was so damn tired, I went back to my room and slept.
Evening Rahasya came and I woke up.
I woke up. I saw her, she came straight to me and gave me one tight slap. I was not angry, but I was shocked.
I didn't know what did I do.
What did I do, I asked?
Don't speak with me, she said.

Krissh saw the whole incident, I asked him what happened. He said that maybe she's angry with the selfies or you just left to India without telling anything, he said.

Alright, I'm planning something Krissh, I said.
I just need your help in this. After all, you are completely free and jobless, I said.
Tell me whatever it is, I'll help you, he said.

I"ll speak to the medical director of my company and through his influence, I'll ask him to transfer her to my facility.
After that, I will try to recreate the moment I spent with her in India. I'll take the help of Isabelle too. All I need is to hire some people for my perfect situations, I said.

Okay, I can help with that, I have some contacts for that too, he said.

I Knocked at the door.
May I come in sir, I asked?
Come in Rahul, please take a seat, medical director Dr. Sujay said.
How are you Rahul, What can I do for you, he asked?
Dear sir, I need a favor from you, I said.

I told him the whole story about Rahasya, So could you please transfer her to this facility as even that hospital is a branch of us.

Also am trying to recreate the moment that we spent in India, I said.
Alright, I'll see what I can do about it. And take your time for this, I pray that she gets back all her memory. You have all my support, he said.
I was happy. Immediately I contacted Isabelle.

Isabelle, how are you, I asked?
Damn man! It seems like you forgot about me, no phone calls, no messages. You have landed here and it's been two days and now you remember me, she said.

Come on, Isabelle, you know my work and I was so damn tired when I landed here so I thought to contact you later, I said.

Well, Krissh called and said about your arrival. And most of all where is the treat, She asked?
What are you talking about? I just came back from India, so why treat, I asked?
Oh come on, You started to construct a house and you are not even bothered to tell me, Anyway, what's up, she asked?
I have a plan to bring back Rahasya's memories.
So I discussed the plans with her. I need you to meet up tonight, we will start our first plan, I said.
Alright Rahul, as you say, she said.

Hello, Isabelle. Come let's speak over a cup of coffee, I said.
Krissh was sitting beside her.
Isabelle, I need you to arrange a water tanker filled up.
Why do you need a water tanker with eyes wide open, she asked?
I need to make rain, I said.

Rahul, I remember your story but I don't think this will work. This is Australia for god's sake, not India, she said.
I think she's right, Krissh said.

Okay, Am out of options, What shall I do? you guys suggest me some ideas, I said.
Okay, I have some ideas, hope it works, she said.
Am all ears, I said.

I have a friend, I need you to take her out for a date in the presence of Rahasya.

But first, I need you to start from a bouquet shop.
It's simple.
The owner of the bouquet shop is my friend.
She's the person you are going to take out for a date,
she said.

But what makes this to bring back her memories, I
asked?
Let me finish idiot, she said.
See, when she sees you speaking to my friend in a
romantic way, taking her out and enjoying with her,
she will start to feel jealous.
This jealous will be the start of bringing back her
memories.
You got to act well buddy, she said.
Alright, let's do it as you say, I said.

(28)

The next day, Rahasya was leaving for work. She was waiting at the bus stand. Isabelle arranged everything with her friend, so I just need to follow what Isabelle said to me.
I walked in front of Rahasya and I pretended as if I didn't see her.

I had a Bluetooth earpiece so that Isabelle was watching me from the hideout and guiding me. I walked to that bouquet shop which was just beside the bus stand.
Dear, can you make a bouquet so beautiful that any girl in Australia should fall for it, I said.
Sure, sir, she said.
She made a bouquet and it was so beautiful. It was made out of roses. She gave me the bouquet.

I gave the bouquet to the florist. This bouquet is for you. You look so beautiful. If I asked you out on a date, Would you join, I asked?
with both the hands on her mouth, she said yes.

This whole scene was watched by Rahasya. She was pissed off.
We both then disappeared from the scene.

Next day, the medical director called me.
Rahul, I have arranged for her to work in our facility. I have informed her and that facility. I have

informed the memo that on the account of shortage of staff she's joining here.
I informed this to Isabelle.

Isabelle's next plan was at a party, a ball.
Isabelle said to Krissh and Rahasya that we are going to a party.
She invited them too.

We all went to the party. It was a couple party where all the couples wear masks and then dance together.
We went inside, Krissh and Isabelle started to dance together. I sat for a drink and Rahasya was left over and she sat alone at the table. A woman approached me with a mask on her face. I couldn't recognize her.

Rahasya was seeing this.
What a young handsome man like you doing here sitting all alone, she asked?

I just came for a drink, I said. She touched my hand and slowly pulled me towards her. She came closer and leaned front and whispered in my ear. Dance with me now, Am with Isabelle.

Immediately she pulled me aside and started to dance. Rahasya saw this. I could see some difficulty on her face. She was struggling to sit in one place.
Finally, after 15 minutes she came and ordered a drink. I was shocked to see Rahasya drinking.

I was watching her and after a few minutes, she started to drink for 3 to 4 glasses. Immediately I said this to Isabelle. I went ahead and checked on her.
She was drunk and started to scold me very badly. Isabelle interfered and asked me to move as she will handle the situation.

The mystery Angel disappeared, later Isabelle said it's her friend who danced with me. We came out and booked a cab and reached home.
Rahasya was not in the state to stand, she was continuously omitting. The next day she woke up. She had a very bad headache, it was the hangover. I went and knocked on her door and gave her hot tea. She didn't speak anything.

Lie down, I have informed the authorities. Don't worry about the office, I said.
She didn't speak anything. Please speak something, I said.
She didn't even see my face.

She laid down and then I massaged her head with balm. She closed her eyes slowly.
After a few minutes, I boiled the water and with an old towel, I dipped in the water and then kept on her head.
Ahhhh! she screamed in pain.

Am sorry, Am sorry, I said.
Then I made sure that the heat is reduced.
She closed her eyes and slept.

I stayed back home. I started to cook for her.
Krissh was watching tv.
I cooked and went into the room, Asked her to brush her teeth and she was ready.
I served breakfast on the bed. After eating, she cleaned the house, washed the dishes and went to take a shower. Then she went back to her room and started writing a journal in a new diary.

That day I called Isabelle and told what happened earlier that morning.
She said that it's the starting stage of love, I laughed out loud.

I called appa.
How are you appa, I asked?
Am fine Rahul, How's the construction going on, I asked?
They are done with the roof, It's molded. The house is getting constructed faster than I thought, he said.

I asked how are amma and my brother. Then I hung up my phone.
Later Krissh called Isabelle and asked her to come to the house to speak about the next plan.

She came in the evening and Rahasya was asleep.
Isabelle and I were standing in the balcony. Krissh made hot tea and banana bajji.

Now, Rahul, let's talk about the next plan.
location is your own hospital. The plan is a patient will approach you.

She will come for X-ray. As it's a lady patient, and there will be no other female staff on your floor, So you will inform them to send a sister immediately.

That sister who is sent will be Rahasya. Now, once she is done with the position, you will go inside to check inside. Eventually, this patient will start to flirt with you.

She will kiss you on the cheeks. You should fight and start a scene. You should shout at this patient and at the same time you should tell that patient about Rahasya and how you love her.
This will be seen by Rahasya and then she might regain her memory and will start falling for you.

It was perfectly planned and when I turned back, I saw Rahaysa standing right behind us and hearing our plan. She was crying.
She came and gave me a tight slap.
How could you? how could you all do this to me, she asked?
Isabelle, I trusted you with all my heart.
And what about you Krissh, I've treated you like my own brother. You pay me back with pain, she said.

Rahasya, It's not like that, Isabelle said.
Please, Rahasya, let me explain, Krissh said.
I don't want to hear anything from anybody. Just leave me alone, she said. Am going back to India, she said.
I stood there without uttering a word.

She started to pack. I went inside.

Please Rahasya, trust me. It's not what you think, I said.

Trust you? After all the stupid things you did how can I trust you, she asked?

Please, Rahasya, Don't go. I love you so much, I said.

Well, I fucking hate you, she said.

I don't want to see your face again, she said.

She was crying badly. She made some calls and after that, she left.

I followed her till airport and I begged her but still, she didn't forgive me. She just left that day and disappeared.

<u>**(India)**</u>
<u>ACT 8: Krissh and Isabelle's marriage</u>

(29)

Four years later…..
Krissh brought Isabelle to India, He told his parents about his love.

At first, they didn't accept as she was out of the league.

But later he convinced them and somehow everything was done.

The marriage was fixed. It all happened within the blink of an eye.

He sent me an invitation and invited me, At that time I was transferred to New Zealand and I bought myself a home. I was already half settled.

It's been over four years, I didn't get any calls or messages. It was like she didn't exist. She stayed only in my memories.

I flew to India, along with me I brought a colleague of mine Andrea. Krissh sent me a vehicle to pick me up and her from Devanahalli international airport in Bengaluru.

Krissh's sister Tanisha came along with her driver to pick me up in Jaguar.

How are you dear, I asked Minnu, It's Tanisha's nickname

I'm awesome bro, how about you? How's Australia, she asked?

Can't you even call and check on me if am alive or not? It's not fair! she said.

Oh sorry, Who is this, she asked?

She's Andrea, my colleague from New Zealand. She always wanted to visit India, so I brought her with me, I said.

Oh! I thought you guys were married, I'm sorry, she said.

No, It's okay. Don't ask sorry, Andrea said.

I love India, I always had a dream to visit India but I don't know anybody here.

At the right time Rahul asked me and here I am, she said.

After a few minutes.......

I'm actually settled in New Zealand, Auckland, I said.

After Rahasya left Australia............ I paused.

It was very hard for me to work there. So I bought a home in New Zealand and started working there, I also do part-time Radio jockey.

Damn! you have changed, seems like you have become New Zealand celebrity, Minnu said.

I smiled at her. Nothing like that Minnu, It's just living you know, I said.

Yeah! but still, I'm really sorry about what happened to you and Rahasya, she said.

Chill dear, It's nothing. Shit happens, I said.

But still, I love her so much. It's been almost four years and I never even thought of getting married to another person, I said.

Don't worry brother, whatever happens, it happens for good, she said.

I smiled at her.

Minnu took us to her house, It was huge, It was like a palace.

There were three Rottweilers at the entrance with security guards. Each and every vehicle were been checked. There was a huge place just for vehicle parking.

There were CCTV's all over the compounds, The house was named Sri Krishna Krupa. It was well protected, I felt like I was inside the White House.

As soon as they saw minnu, they saluted her and let us in.

Krissh came out. He was having two bodyguards, they were carrying two rifles and a sidearm. They looked huge and perfectly bodybuilt.

The lion is back, he said. He hugged me and then saw Andrea.

How are you Andrea, he asked?

I'm fine Mr. Krissh, by the way, do you know me, she asked?

Of course, Rahul said everything about you, he said.

Well, come inside. Let's have tea and then you guys go fresh up. I'll arrange the breakfast, he said.

Krissh took us up to the rooms.

Andrea fresh up soon, We are going to have a party, he said.

After a few minutes, I called Krissh in my room, when I pulled him inside, those two bodyguards started to push me.

Hey! it's okay, He's my family, he said.
Sorry, sir, they said.
You can wait outside, I'll be needing some privacy, he said.
They waited outside as he came in. Am really sorry brother for this stupid scene.

It's okay Krissh, but how........... he paused?
Well, after Rahasya left India, We came to India after a week, you know that right, he said.
After that, I had to come to my sister's dance program, It was a huge program.
Every VIP's were present there.
Director's and producers everybody had attended that program and few were my sister's mentors.

My sister suggested me to act in a movie, I wasn't interested, but due to her force, I said yes.
After that, I invested 10 lakhs and one of my sister's director directed the movie with the senior people of the industry. Once the movie was released it was a hit. Every theatre was full.

It was a complete chaos everywhere. It was globally released and it was dubbed in every language.

I don't know how I became a hit, I thought it will flop, but it turned out to be one of the best movies. A lot of awards were given to me. Slowly I got myself into politics, I thought that the more the money I can do something good for the society.
I stood up for election. When I got money because of my movies, I was rich there. But later I realized that some of my money can be used for the welfare of the people. So basically when I was a hit, people knew me and they made me win the election.

I took care of things here in my jurisdiction. I gave all the needs and I made sure that nobody should sleep hungry, no children should miss out on the education, I started paying fees for the orphans for their education.

When this was seen by the other MLA's, they hired people to kill me. I had been attacked twice. Thank god, I was saved.

From then on, I made myself secure. No more than 10 feet a person should stand. When the service for the people was seen by the government, They promised me that even they will also take care of me. So that's how this is, he said.

That's wonderful Krissh, I'm very happy for you, I said.
Why didn't you call me man, he asked?
your mobile number has also been changed, he said.
You completely disappeared.
By the way, Rahasya is here, he said.

I opened my eyes wide and asked him What?
You two are not together huh, he asked?
No brother, I said, It's been almost four years, I said.

Woah! I thought you called her and spoke and everything was alright. Am sorry brother, he said.
Chill brother, It's okay, I said.
Well, I'll go down, Freshen up, and my sis was talking something about you being a Radio Jockey, Is it true, he asked?
Yeah! I said.
Well, I will speak to the directors regarding you and will make a movie, he said.
Let's talk later about this business, now you freshen up and come down, Rahasya's there.
Try to speak with her and also there's a party so hurry up, he said.
Hmm bro, Okay I will, I said.

After my shower, I put on something like a party wear. I went and knocked on Andrea's room, she didn't open. So I thought I'll meet her up downstairs.

I went down and there I saw Isabelle.
Hello Rahul, she came towards me and hugged.
It's been ages seeing your face, how are you, she asked?

I thought you forgot me, I tried calling you but the number said it's invalid. You just disappeared from us, What happened, she asked?
I smiled at her.

Krissh told me everything, Am sorry about that. Rahul, I'm very busy as it's my engagement so I gotta go, buddy, she said.

No, It's okay. You can leave, I'll take care. By any chance have you seen Andrea, The one who I came with, I asked?
She's just behind you, by the way, thank you for coming or else I would have hunted you down to death, she said.

Well, look who's here, William's entry.
How are you Rahul, Long time no see, he asked?
I smiled at him.
Where's your girlfriend, he asked?

Isabelle saw this and she ran and came towards us.
William's, don't ask that. It's not the right time now, she said.
Sorry, Rahul, He's still the same old idiot, she said and pulled him and went.

I turned myself back to see Andrea and she was speaking to Rahasya.
I stood there like a carved statue from stone. She was so beautiful, She wore a red gown with golden borders. She was like an angel.
She was laughing with Andrea. I went near her.
Oh where have you been Rahul, Andrea asked?

Well, Rahul, this is Rahasya, and Rahasya this is Rahul, She introduced.

We looked into each other's eyes, She was carrying
a child.

hmm! finally, even she's married, I thought to
myself.
I shook hands with her.
How are you Rahul, she asked?
Am good Rahasya, how are you, I asked?
Am good Rahul.
So how's your life going on, she asked?
It's good, simple.

Suddenly Krissh announced.
Everybody come forward, Ladies and gentleman, I
thank you for each and everyone who is attending
my party and those who will attend my wedding
with Isabelle.
It's an honor to enjoy my day with all of you. Have
a wonderful evening ladies and gentlemen. Let the
party begin, he said.

She was taking care of that child. That child was
crying continuously and she was convincing him.
Andrea asked me to dance with her. I said yes.
We were dancing slowly, but my eyes were on
Rahasya. She was seeing me too, but when she was
looking at me, I was pretending to involve in dance.

(30)

Later that night we all sat together for dinner. After dinner, I went to the bartender, Krissh was having a mini bar inside his house as a part of the party.
I asked the bartender to get me one full bottle of Scotland Chivas Regal. Sir, but this stuff is strong, he said.
Just give me brother, I need to drink and spill my pain which I've kept inside for almost four years, I said.

Being a brother from another mother, will you please give me, I asked?
Take it, sir, he said.
Dear sir, If you don't mind will you tell me why are you drinking, he asked?

Love failure brother, don't love anybody. It is the easiest way to kill yourself every second with AK 47 and then again live. Instead of loving it's better to die as soon as we are born. Don't love anybody brother, I said.

Later I went to the terrace and started drinking that whole bottle. I was drunk, William's had come upstairs to smoke and he saw me.

What are you doing here, he asked?
Bro, I want to ask you one thing. Did you love Isabelle truly?

I didn't but when I lost her I came to know the value of her, he said.

I remember that day Rahasya too came in search of me.
I loved Rahasya so much Wiiliam's. If I was playing with girls it would have been fun I guess. I loved her so deeply. I was ready to give everything to her. When she lost the memory I thought I lost her.

But still, with all my effort I tried to regain back her memories. I set sail my heart in search of her. She left me and went to William's, I said and started to cry. I wept like a baby. I couldn't hold my breath.
Now she's gone, I said.

Brother, I understand your pain. I stood there once a long time ago. It's painful.
I wasn't rich that day, Now am rich but not to the level of Krissh. I thought she might come when am being rich.
But no, she didn't. I want her to be happy even if she's married to other.

But when I think for a second that I'm not the person who is not married to her, It breaks my heart William, I said. I don't know what happened after that. I fell unconscious.

I woke up the next day in my Rahasya's room. It was not clear what happened to me and how did I end up there.

I'm sorry Rahasya, I thought It's my room and I might have come in and slept yesterday.

It's okay Rahul and you didn't come in, I and William made you sleep here.
I didn't say a word, I woke up and went to my room and took shower and attended the wedding.

There were a lot of people at his wedding. Isabelle was dressed in a beautiful golden saree and Krissh in a normal traditional wear.
There were cops and bodyguards all over the ceremony. The whole film industry was present for his wedding. Every politician was there at the ceremony.

Everybody had their own bodyguards. There were bomb squads and dogs. The place was totally secured. I started giving cool drinks to the people. Krissh saw this and ordered me not to do stupid stuff.

Rahasya was watching me. It was so painful to see her. Loved her to the core but couldn't get married to her.
Soon the Muhurtam time approached and people started to bless the couple.
They both looked awesome. Even though Isabelle was a Christian the marriage was done in Hindu tradition, After all, even Isabelle was forcing Krissh to get married in Hindu style.

Krissh tied the knot to Isabelle and they walked the seven steps around the fire. Finally, the couple was married.

Rahasya eyes were filled with tears. She looked at me in despair. I didn't know what was going in her mind. She wiped her tears. Krissh was very happy. His parents were behind him. They were so happy. Krissh and Isabelle fell to their feet.

Amma, Isabelle said.
Krissh's mother turned back. Did you just call me amma, she asked?
Yes, amma, Isabelle said.
I want to tell you something, she said.
Tell me, Isabelle, amma said.

No matter what happens, No matter what problem arises, I will never mistreat you, I will take care of you and appa, I will always be the same old Isabelle to you amma, she said.

But why did you tell this suddenly dear, she asked?
Amma, when I came here, Krissh once took me to the old age home, There were so many people who were cast out by their own children once they are married or that might be one of the reasons.

90% of the people who were put there was because of women. When I saw that my heart melted. how can they do such a cruel thing to their own parents? As am an orphan, for me you are the parents and you are gods to me, she said.

146

Krissh's mother started to cry, First, Krissh was not listening to this, later he saw her speaking and when he heard what she told, his eyes were filled with tears.

Then the photo shoot started. Some were hungry so most of them were eating. I was sitting in the front row.

There were media and his wedding was broadcast on live on every channel.

Krissh saw me. he asked me to come up as he wanted to speak.

What happened brother, Why the long face, he asked?

It's nothing bro, I said.

Idiot fellow, did you speak with Rahasya, he asked?

No, I said.

Speak with her man, he said.

Please, will you book a cab for me to go to the airport, I want to leave India as soon as I can, I said.

What the hell are you speaking, you shouldn't go anywhere for the next 2 months.

Don't worry I already made arrangements with your company where you are working and also I sent some of my people to look after your house for another 2 months, he said.

What the hell, when were you planning to tell me this, I asked.

Now sit down, I also brought you some clothes and I've made arrangements for Andrea too, Everything will be taken care of, he said.

I was shocked, I had no other choice, I had to listen to him.

Andrea heard this.
What?
Krissh, I should go back, I can't stay here, she said.
No dear, At least for me you should be here with Isabelle. I have many plans for you and Rahul. I'll take you to places and we will enjoy.
And also I have some important work with Rahul's life, he said.

Will you stay at least for Rahul, he asked?
If it's for Rahul then I'll stay, she said.
As our turn came for the photoshoot, I, Andrea and Rahasya took a photo with Isabelle and Krissh.
Andrea, If you don't mind, can I take another photo with Rahul and Rahasya separately, he asked?
Chill brother, I can understand, she said and moved away.
I stood with Isabelle and Rahasya stood with Krissh. The photoshoot was done.

We didn't have a proper smile on our face. As it was their wedding we faked our smile for the photoshoot.
Later that night we had dinner together and standing for most of the hours continuously Isabelle and Krissh were tired.
They went to sleep and I had no sleep so I went to the terrace and spent my time there alone. I had so many things to tell Rahasya.
I decided to tell these all to Rahasya then and there.

I called her but she didn't answer my calls. I thought she was sleeping.
So I didn't disturb her.

The following day, William's bid us goodbye and he left India. He was handling some huge business so he had to go. When he knocked on my door early morning by 06:00 to inform me that he's leaving I woke up.

Once I woke up my sleep just went. Krissh was already up and he was in his office. As soon as he saw me, he came out and said something about a trip to Manali. I thought there might be some personal work of his so I kept quiet.
Rahasya came downstairs, she looked straight into my eyes.

Hey Rahasya, We are leaving to Manali tonight, he said.
Okay, have a safe journey, she said.
Arrey! It's not just us, we all are going to Manali tonight, you, me, Isabelle, Rahul, Andrea. Let's enjoy some moments there, he said.

But............. she paused.
No buts, I'll spend on everything for you guys. I just want you guys to be with me, he said.
In fact, everything is arranged for us, he said.
Hmmm okay, she said.

Krissh, where is Andrea, he asked?
She's in her room, I said.

Well, wake her up, he said.

No, Let her sleep, After all, it's just 06:45. She might not have the practice of getting up so soon, Rahasya said.

Oh yeah! I didn't think about that, he said.

Where is Isabelle, is she still sleeping, she asked?

No, she's already up and she's in the kitchen making tea for us, he said.

Well, I'll join her, she said and went in.

after a few minutes, she and Isabelle came. Rahasya gave me and Krissh tea and Isabelle went upstairs to wake up Krissh's parents to give them tea.

Krissh took the newspaper and we sat in the garden outside. It was chilly in the morning at the same time the sun was rising. That warm and chilly feel in the morning with a hot cup of tea was so awesome. It was like heaven.

Krissh, Do I really need to come, I asked?

You have to Rahul. It's my wish, he said.

Alright, I'll come, I said.

Andrea woke up and I told about this trip and she was ready to go with me.

In the noon I called amma.

How are you Amma, I asked?

Am fine Rahul, How's Krissh, How did the wedding go, she asked?

Am good, the wedding went well ma.

By the way, Am leaving to north India tonight, Krissh asked me to come. And am also staying here for the next two months, I said.

Next two months? Are you joking, she asked?

no, ma, Krissh has arranged everything in New Zealand for my house and he has spoken to my company too. They said they will pay me for the next two months, I said.

I'll come home once I come back from north India, I said.

Suddenly why are you going there, she asked?

I don't know, It's a normal trip. He has booked tickets for everyone, I said.

Be careful, be safe, she said.

Okay ma, Don't worry, I'll hang up the phone, I said.

Pack your things, buddy and ask Andrea to get ready too.

Rahasya, Even you too, Krissh said.

Krissh told he had booked till Delhi. From there we were to go by car or bus, I was not sure. In the evening at 04:30 We all got ready and waited for him. A car was arranged and it was a black Hummer. It was so huge. We all sat and left for the airport.

Usually, people go to the Devanahalli international airport. but we were at the old airport in HAL.

Krissh, What work do you have here, I asked?

Buddy, this is the place where we will board the flight, he said.

But this is not in use, Only VIP's get down here when they come, I said.

You just come, I'll tell you everything, he said.

We were dropped off by car inside the airport on the runway near to the airlift.
We all got down and his bodyguards were loading our bags in an airlift.
Well, Rahul, this is my own private airlift, he said.
I opened my eyes wide with half mouth open and looked at him.

Are you kidding me, I asked?
nope, he said.
Then why did you lie about the tickets, I asked?
Just for fun, he said.
We boarded the airlift at 05:30 and it was like a mini palace inside.
There were big sofa's, a table, a fridge, a mini bar, two air hostess, one snooker table. It was built in royalty.
Take your seats, he said. He spoke to the captain in a phone. Please take off within 5 minutes, he said.
Opposite to me, Rahasya sat.

Andrea sat beside me, Of course, she doesn't know about my love for Rahasya.
Isabelle and Krissh were together, four bodyguards were with us, they were sitting separately.
Airhostess helped us by putting the seat belts.

fasten your seatbelts. We will be taking off within a minute, wishing a happy married life Mr. Krissh and Mrs. Isabelle Krissh. we also wish you a happy journey and have a safe flight. We will be landing Delhi by 08:00.
And they took off.

<u>ACT 9: New Delhi</u>

(31)

Soon we landed at Indira Gandhi international airport in New Delhi, It was approximately 08:00 in the evening. It was an awesome flight, Krissh kept the environment alive, there was partying, dancing, storytelling, and we also played snooker.
We had a wonderful time. After landing, Krissh had already booked The Leela palace and it was 28 km away from the airport. So there were already 3 Rolls Royce waiting for us outside.

Krissh and Isabelle with a bodyguard were sitting in one car. I, Rahasya and Andrea and one bodyguard sat in one car and two bodyguards sat in another car behind us.
We soon arrived at "the Leela."
It was a huge palace, there were two women dressed in their uniform. They welcomed us with a namaste.
Our bags were unloaded by he bodyguards and some of their men. The room was a suite. It was so huge. Three suites were given. One suite was with three rooms. In one room Isabelle and Krissh went. Three extra rooms suites were given to me, Andrea and Rahasya.
One more suite was given to the bodyguards.

The suite was exactly like a home, After 10 minutes welcome drinks were provided to us and Krissh asked us to take shower and get back down for dinner.

We went down for dinner and Krissh and Isabelle were waiting for us.

During the flight, Andrea and Rahasya were together so they were together all the time.

We sat all together in a huge dining hall. Krissh asked us to order our wishes and we ordered some good non-veg. After eating there were some programs given to the customers. We all sat there and were discussing the trip. It was a good dinner though. Krissh asked us to wake up early in the morning as we will start the journey early.

Andrea and Rahasya stayed awake in the other room throughout the night. They slept around 03:00.

I was waking up now and then due to their stories and laughs.

Andrea woke me up when it was time.

Sorry, Rahul, she said.

Why?

We were disturbing your sleep, so.............. she paused.

It's okay. Am used to it, I said.

I went for a walk downstairs to admire the day beauty of "The Leela". Of course, that's what I thought but it was still dark. I went and stood near the entrance and it was chilly. One of the attendants offered me tea.

As I stood there, a hand was kept on my right shoulder from behind. I turned back to see and it was Rahasya.

Wow! she was totally ready to go. It seemed like I was the one who left out to take bath. She wore a red shirt, hands folded and a short knicker, she had this wonderful muffler too tied up around her neck.

What are you doing here? go get ready soon, she said.

It's beautiful here in the morning and chilly too, so I came to spend some time here, I said.

That's wonderful, but I suggest you go now before Krissh comes, He will blast you, she said.

I laughed out loud. It's been days I've laughed out this loud, I said.

Rahul...................... she paused.

Before she was about to tell me something, Andrea called me out loud.

I turned back and Rahasya backed up.

Tell me, Andrea, I said.

Come upstairs soon and get ready, she said.

I saw Rahasya's face and she was completely down.

I went upstairs and took bath. I called amma to check how she's doing and packed everything and went downstairs with the bag and Krissh saw me.

What the hell are you doing man, he asked?

Sorry am late, I said.

No, It's not that Rahul. Why are you bringing the bags, he asked?

It's my bag bro, I told.

No, No, It's the work of our bodyguards. You don't touch anything. You just enjoy this trip. We will be in Manali for 2 days. After this, we will be leaving for Paris soon.

Paris! Rahasya jumped out in wonder.

Well, What about you Rahul, he asked?

Alright, will go, I said.

Then I sat for breakfast. Andrea sat beside me. Rahasya saw this and she just put her head down. She didn't speak anything.

People had their own views so they ordered different varieties of food.

After breakfast, A guy approached me with a feedback form and asked me to fill it out. I filled it with excellence and we all came out.

There were 2 Hummers waiting for us.

We boarded one and the bodyguards boarded the other.

Shridhar who was a bodyguard asked Krissh.

Sir, should I stay with you?

It's no need buddy. Enjoy your trip, have fun. Just make sure you guys are behind us, he said.

Sure, sir, he said and left.

While leaving, Krissh gave some tips to the valet guy and some housekeeping. They gave a box of chocolates and Bouquet for Krissh asking us to visit again.

A young woman aged around 24 approached us.

Dear sir, I didn't recognize you at first. I'm really sorry for disturbing as you're leaving. But can I get a picture with you and also your autograph. My sister loves you so much, sir. Could you please wait for another 5 minutes as she's upstairs, sir. Please, she requested.

The manager came and shouted at her.
It's okay sir, Don't scold her. After all, she's my fan. Once a long time ago even I was a fan. People usually rejected me or pushed me from getting pictures and autographs. I'll wait, Krissh said.
Her sister came. She ran towards Krissh and hugged him. Krissh slowly touched her and looked at her.
You are a cute child, he said.

She started to cry with happiness.
What happened? Why are you crying, he asked.
Sir, I have a request for you. Once you are free will you visit my mother? She's very fond of you. She always wanted to see you, she said.
Okay sure, no problem he said.
They took selfies and autographs.

By the way, Where do you live, he asked?
I live 2 blocks away, she said.
Alright then, Let's see your mother now only, he said.
Both the girls were so excited and they started to arrange a cab.

No, I will come with our vehicle, You sit with us, he said.

With your permission, can I take her with us for a
few minutes, he asked the manager?
Sure, sir, he said.

We all went to where she stayed.
We all got down. People were looking at us. The
place was totally a mess, there were no proper
facilities, no proper roads, It was a slum.
Eventually, we went inside her house. I was
thinking how beautiful these girls are and they did
hotel management by borrowing money from others
and they are working in one of the biggest star
hotels and they are from a poor background.

This is my amma, she showed us to the bedroom
where she was bedridden. She was so sick she
couldn't move her head to see who has come.
Slowly one girl lifted her up and she saw Krissh.
As soon as she saw, tears slowly rolled through her
cheeks. It was so painful to see. He sat with her and
spoke with her. due to sickness, she couldn't even
speak.
I didn't get your name dear, he said.
It's Aradhana, she said.

Okay Aradhana, how much did you pay our college
fees for hotel management, he asked.
Sir, I paid 3 lakhs each for and my sis, she said.
Okay, but how much do you get paid, he asked?
I take home 15,000/-.
15,000/-? what the hell is this?

What about you, he asked the other?

Sir, I get paid 20,000/- per month.
What? damn!
Well, how do you handle the expenses for your mother's health, he asked?
Our both salaries will be spent on her medicines the only sir, we get food from the hotel. We make foods for amma, she said.

Well, how did you repay your fees money, he asked?
They both looked at each other in despair. Well, sir, we are working on that, they said
How much you have paid till now, he asked?
1 lakh sir, she said.

He sat there for almost 5 minutes of thinking something.
They asked us to sit down and they put a mat.
We are really sorry. You are big people and we don't have a chair.

It's okay Aradhana, I said.
Isabelle went inside and was advising them.

After a few minutes, Krissh came.
Shridhar, get me a cheque, he said.
sir, he said and gave the cheque.
He wrote 20 lakh rupees and signed the cheque and gave it to Aradhana.

Sir, I don't need this from you. We wished you to meet amma and that's the happiest ever, she said.

Now, don't reject this. I want you to repay whoever it is you borrowed and the remaining money is for you and your mother medical expenses, he said.

Call the HR of "The Leela", he said to a bodyguard.
Yes, this is Krissh from Karnataka, he said.
I need you to raise the salary of Ms. Aradhana and just a minute, he said.
What is your name ma, he asked?
Aroopana sir, she said.

Yeah and Aroopana he continued.
I want them to take home 90,000/- to 1 lakh per month, he said.
And I repeat both of them.
I think I shouldn't call you again regarding this, he said.
As soon as he kept the call, they both received a message informing they are promoted and their pay is increased to 1 lakh.

He arranged an ambulance and admitted their mother and arranged for a person to take care of the things and discounted for 70% of the bill amount for them.

They both started to cry and fell at his feet.
No, No, Please get up. Don't cry dear ones.
Take me as your own brother, I said. They hugged Krissh together and Krissh started to wipe his tears.
It was such a lovely moment.

If you come to Bengaluru, I'll definitely arrange a home for you guys. I can transfer both of you to the Bengaluru Leela palace. and you can run a family there, he said.

We will definitely sir, We needed a change, they said.
Krissh gave his number and we bid goodbye and we left for Manali.

(32)

It was a long journey, The distance was approximately 500 to 560km. We went through NH 44, before entering the Himachal Pradesh border it was so hot, but once we crossed the border they switched off all the AC's and we opened the window and it was completely cold. We went via Shimla. We stopped at Shimla to have some drinks and snacks. Everybody was so sleepy.

I love long travels, a window seat, and headphones or earphones will make my journey complete. Krissh got down, he wanted to piss so badly. He asked me out.
Rahul, Am so freaking urgent to pass, join with me, he said.

Andrea laughed out loud.
Oh, come on! this is boys thing, he said.
Well, I joined him and it was very cold. The total atmosphere changed within a fraction of seconds and it was snowing a bit.
Rahasya was seeing snow for the first time. She was excited, jumping and dancing around.
We finished our business and we went to have something hot.

Krissh ordered hot chocolates for everybody.
Rahasya was excited of snow and she took the hot chocolate and she went out to have.

Krissh gave a cue to one of his bodyguards to go behind her and take care of her. So one of the guys went to look after her and he too was drinking hot chocolate.

One of the north Indian started to use abusive words and taunt Rahasya. I stood up to go and fight. Krissh told me to sit down and calm. One of the bodyguards stood beside her and he just showed his sidearm to that guy. He went away. Immediately Krissh said to catch him.
He ran and caught that guy.

Krissh was sitting calmly. I mean who can sit like that when somebody's been harassed. He pulled that guy and brought to us. Immediately people surrounded and two of the bodyguard was protecting Krissh and one more was protecting us.

Krissh got up from his place and he went towards that north Indian and he slapped twice. It was a very hard one.
Say sorry to her, he said.
He refused.
Do you know who I am, he asked?
He didn't speak anything.
Andrea and Isabelle were speaking to each other. They looked calm too.

He shouted at him in his bass voice and gave one more.
He started to beg her and tell sorry.
Shridhar, call the local police, he said.

Within 5 minutes the police arrived. As soon as they came, they saluted him.

How may I help you, sir, one of the cops asked Krissh.

I don't want to file any case against him. But if he's committed any crime in your jurisdiction or any other places and if he's wanted then he's all yours, he said.

Sir, he's a local pick-pocketer. We have been trying to catch him for 2 years. He just slips through our hands, they said.

Sir, you can file a case on him, one of the cops said.

No, I think he's learned the lesson, he said.

While leaving, he turned back and said to him, You can steal all the money in this world. That's a choice you make, but never ever harass a woman or a girl.

next time if I get to know that your harassing or mocking a woman. I'll make sure to cut your manhood and walked away silently.

Let's enjoy come on Rahasya, he said.

She was crying and weeping continuously.

Krissh looked at me and gave a signal to convince her.

I went near her. Ammu, don't cry, I said.

I can understand this but Krissh helped us out, I said.

Krissh interfered, Rahasya when he saw you in trouble, he immediately got up with anger and went to blast that guy you know. It was me who asked him to sit calmly and will handle the situation, he said.

Now cheer up Rahasya, I said.
If he had touched you? in case if he had touched you, he repeated. Then I would have broken his hand and hospitalized him, I said.
Ah! this is enough for Rahasya. What a beautiful pair, he said.

She turned her face and gave a look at him.
Alright, chill, I am out of here, he said and he started laughing.

Everybody was sleeping throughout the journey. Of course, it was a long and tiresome journey. I don't sleep during journeys. I sat in the front seat and started to speak with the driver. He was a Kannadiga from Karnataka. But he knew Malayalam too. He was good at it.

What is your name sir, I asked?
My name is Nikhil sir, he replied.
Well, how long are you into this driving business, I asked?
Am driving since 15 years sir, he said.
15 years? that's really a long way, I said.
Actually, I've been a driver for Krissh sir since 3 and a half years, he said.

When he became a film actor, he wanted to appoint a driver, and I used to be a cab driver before that. So he gave me an offer. he said that he will pay me

50,000 per month. I mean who will give such a huge amount of money per month. Nowadays even software engineer don't earn as much as me, he said. That's true, I said.

By the way, are you married, I asked?
Yes, sir, I have two kids. One is studying in 5th and the other one is in 10th. Krissh sir is my guardian angel. He's the one who pays my kids their fees. He loves the students who study well, So he started donating money for children's funds, he said.

That's wonderful, I said.
Sir, are you married, he asked?
I paused for a minute and looked at him. Well, no sir, not yet, I said.
But sir, you are well settled and you are from New Zealand. How come you are still single, He asked.
Did you love somebody, he asked?
I laughed out loud. I was in love, I mean I still love her. But it's too late now, I said.
Sir, I don't know what is the problem you had faced or facing but I would love to tell you one thing. It's never too late for anything, he said.
I paused for a moment and I asked him to turn on the music.

I looked at the rearview mirror and saw Rahasya staring at me. I pretended as if I didn't see her.
As it was late, even I was feeling sleepy. By the time I slept Isabelle woke up and she was busy speaking to the driver.

We arrived at Apple Valley resorts in Kullu. Isabelle woke me up. I was so tired.

Wake up Rahul, Isabelle said.
Welcome to Apple Valley, he said. We are going to visit the Rohtang pass.

I got up and it was freezing outside. We all went to our respective rooms, I started to freshen up.

I went out to a nearby liquor shop and bought myself a Rum. I was drinking early morning by 7:00.
Krissh saw this and he started to blast me.
I told him to get ready fast and I sat downstairs on the couch using free wifi.

Rahasya came down. She sat next to me and it was weird. I couldn't speak anything.
I stared at my phone and saw her face through my phone screen reflection.
Rahul, she said.
I looked towards her and suddenly Isabelle came.
Rahasya, let's drink a hot cup of tea, she said.
Rahul, join us, she said.
I just had a bottle of Rum, I said.
What the hell, she asked?
What is wrong with you? how can you drink a bottle of liquor early morning, she asked?
Isabelle sat there and stared at my face.
I want to tell you guys something, she said.

Andrea was coming downstairs, Hi everybody, she said.
Isabelle dropped the matter then and there only.
Krissh came down. Let's start the enjoyment, he said.
Andrea and Rahasya boarded the vehicle.
Oye! beautiful ladki's, he said. We are going by walk, not by vehicle, he said.
They started to laugh with embarrassment. They came behind us.

We went to a nearby river, It was a small stream but powerful enough to pull a man and drown. The current was powerful. There was a wild river crossing, A rope tied to each end and then one cross the river just with the help of their hands but the body will be tied to the rope so that they won't fall into the river or drown themselves.

Isabelle is an adventure person. As soon as she saw this, she said she wants to try.
Eventually, I tried. We were tied up and while crossing he just let loose the rope. I was put deep inside the river and it was freaking freezing. When I was pulled up I started to shiver. I was all wet.
Krissh and Rahasya started laughing loudly. Andrea was mocking me.
It was so cold, I couldn't walk, I went back to the room and changed my dress and came back to join them.

From there we went boating to a nearby resort. had some drinks, played badminton.

Krissh went and brought our vehicles. he wanted to go to Rohtang pass.

We all boarded and it was almost 1 and a half hour journey. We stopped now and then to see the beautiful scenery created by God. Two eyes weren't enough to see the beauty of nature in the Himalayas. There were suicide points.

There were waterfalls. Andrea was completely surprised to see the beauty she said. That's why people call, "Incredible India."
We started to clap for her. In some places as she was a foreigner, they asked us to pay extra. But due to Krissh's power, it was the same for her too.

We got down and had Maggie. It was so hot and tasty because of that lovely climate nobody couldn't refuse it.
We had black tea. Comparing to the south it is so expensive in the north, especially in the Himalayan regions.
They charged 100 bucks just for on plate of Maggie. But in the south, it's just 11 bucks.

From there we arranged horses to ascend the mountain.
Each horse could carry two people.

Behind me, Rahasya sat. Andrea sat separately where her horse was tied up to ours. Krissh and Isabelle sat in one horse together and all together we ascended the mountain.

We reached the top. There was still 30km to reach the mountain peak. But the horses could reach only to that point, as the oxygen level started decreasing. It was so freezing, they provided woolen clothes so thick it weighed around 10kgs, They also provided boots, gloves, and caps so that we can play with the snow. The Rohtang pass was visible. It was so beautiful.

We stayed there for an hour and then we needed to get back down. There were paragliding at that time and Isabelle said that we can descent down with a parachute.
Andrea went first, Followed by Krissh and Isabelle.
Rahasya joined me and we both were ready to go down the mountain.

Once we were in the air, We could feel our own heartbeat. It was so quiet, It was freezing though. We glided through the air, Rahasya caught my hand. It was warm. She shouted at the top of her voice to express her happiness.

Rahul, I want to tell you something, she said.
I didn't utter a word. I was quite.
She was about to say something, I yelled Krissh. It was our landing moment.
Krissh was already waiting at the paraglide base.
He was waving and I waved at him too.

We landed and then in moved away from Rahasya. I was scared, After all, I lost her. What more I have in this world to lose, I thought.

I went straight to a liquor shop which was there and I bought myself a Bacardi and started drinking that.

Isabelle saw that and she started to shout at me.

Andrea started to shout at me.

Please ladies, What did I do, I asked?

You keep drinking. This is the 2nd liquor from the morning and it's not even noon yet, Andrea said.

Am sorry, I said.

Forget her man, Andrea said.

Isabelle looked at her and me.

Okay, drop this matter, now let's enjoy the day, Isabelle said.

Rahasya was staring everybody with confusion. She was staring at me. I could see that pain in her face.

Loving her so much and not being with her was so much pain to me. I couldn't handle or control the pain. It was like walking on fire, I went aside and started to cry.

Later Andrea came to me, hugged me.

When Andrea hugged me, Rahasya saw that and walked away to the other side.

Sorry for shouting at you, please don't cry. It's for your sake am telling Rahul. If you keep drinking that stuff 5 to 10 bottles per day continuously it will affect your health within a month. you will be in pain Rahul, she said.

Okay, Sorry Andrea if I had hurt you earlier, I said.

Chill idiot, she said.

Isabelle came and she started to convince me.

Rahul, I can understand how you feel. Give some time brother, I'll help you out soon, she said.
It's okay Isabelle. I can understand your concern but she's already married, I said.
Nooooooooooo, she jumped out of excitement.
She isn't married.

I looked at her face in shock.
Behind her, Rahasya was standing and I didn't notice her at that time.
But, When I saw her the first day at your house she had a child, I said.
No Rahul, It was some other child. She isn't married. Even I thought she was married when she first arrived here. Because I had heard about her marriage arrangement after she disappeared from Australia. But she said there was a family issue so she didn't get married.

When Isabelle said she didn't get married, It fell into her ears and she turned and saw me and I came to know. She walked away from there.
Did she get her memories back, I asked Isabelle?
I don't know Rahul, I have asked her and she always changed the subject.
I want to know if she regained all her memories, I said.

Krissh came there, Hey what's the discussion going on here, he asked?
Isabelle gave a look and he was like, Arrey! am just kidding Isabelle.
Babe, Can you do me a favor, Isabelle asked him.

Why are you asking it as a favor? Come on, Am your husband, he said.
I want you to find out whether Rahaysa has got back her old memories or not, she said.
Alright, I can do that. I just need some time with her, that's all, he said.
Okay, she said
.

Well come on, I don't want sad faces. Get your asses and let's enjoy other stuff, he said.
Rahul, You don't keep drinking, We have a party soon, he said.
Isabelle said, oh yeah! then you guys will drink again.

Krissh looked at her with a wide smile on his face.
Babe, It's party, Let's enjoy. Pleaaaasssseee, he said.
Alright alright, But I don't want Rahul to get drunk up, she said.
Yeah! I'll take care of that, he said.

We boarded the cars and went to a nearby hotel.
It was so cold and everybody was hungry, Krissh asked us to order anything that we want. Isabelle started to order varieties of dishes.
Krissh got a phone call and he went outside to answer the call. Andrea was busy watching the view near the window. Rahasya was staring at me. Can I speak to you personally? Isabelle asked Andrea.
Of course, she said. They went outside to talk.

Rahasya, I thought you were married, I said.
No, Rahul. There were some issues, she said.

So, any other guy in your life.......... I paused.
She didn't say anything for a moment.
No, she said.
I couldn't wait, I lost my patience and asked her, Rahasya, I'll ask you a question, please be honest with me, I said.
Anything, she said.
Did you get back your memories, I asked?
She looked at the sky through the window. She didn't answer anything.
Have you married Rahul, She asked?

No, Rahasya.
What about Andrea, she asked?
She's just a colleague Ammu, I said. It came in the flow without my knowledge.
Am sorry, I said immediately.
It's okay, It's been a long time somebody called me that, she said.
Actually, happy to hear, she said.
What are you doing now, Rahul she asked?
Settled in New Zealand, having a country life, doing some part-time entertainment for the people, and upgraded with the same work what I was doing before, I said.
What about you, I asked?
Just doing something for a living, going with the flow of life, she said.

Krissh came, Hello people, am back, he said.
Oh! sorry to disturb you guys, by the way, if you have seen my wife please tell her to meet me, he said.

Hey Krissh, it's okay, sit with us, Rahasya said.
Krissh sat. It's been a long time since we have sat like this together, he said.
Rahasya smiled. I nodded my head.

Andrea came with Isabelle and sat with us.
Where were you, he asked?
I was just observing the nature outside and enjoying tea with Andrea, Isabelle said.
Where are Shridhar and our people, Krissh asked?
They are sitting outside enjoying some smoke, she said.
He yelled out Shridhar.
Yes, sir, he said. You guys order anything you want, he said.

Different dishes arrived and we started to eat.
Suddenly Andrea said, I've been thinking about Rahul's girlfriend.
Isabelle looked at my face, everybody started to stare at each other.
Why? What happened, she asked?
I've been asking Rahul from past 1 year to show his girlfriend's pic. But he always says he doesn't have or he will show me later, she said.

Rahasya looked at Andrea.
Am his girlfriend, she said as she kept a spoon full of soup in her mouth.
I thought I didn't hear properly, Isabelle and Krissh looked at Rahasya with wonder. Andrea choked on her food and started to cough.

Pass the water, Rahasya said and she tapped on her head to make her stop coughing.

After some time, she recovered back and was in a shock she kept watching mine and Rahasya's face continuously.
Are you serious Rahasya, she asked?
Yeah! Why dear? It seems like you couldn't believe me, she said.

Actually, I couldn't believe that Rahul's girl would be so damn beautiful, she said.
Rahasya smiled, I was eating and I didn't utter a word.
Rahul, Why didn't you tell anything about Rahasya, Andrea asked me?
Isabelle looked at Andrea and eyeballed her. She changed the topic by telling something about her hobbies.

After that, we went to a nearby magic show.
Rahasya fell down by mistake and her elbow region was scratched.
Krissh went immediately to catch her. I ran immediately to a nearby medical shop and asked for first aid. I brought it and I washed the wound, applied the cream and tied the bandage.

Rahasya was telling, It's okay Rahul, It's just a scratch. Don't worry about this.
I was so scared I thought she was in so much pain. While putting the bandage she was looking at me like she has never seen me. She was staring at my

eyes. Even though I didn't see her, I could make out her looking at me.

Finally, she said she's fine.
After the magic show, We went straight to the room.
We were sitting all together in the garden around a bonfire and Krissh already organized a party.
The resort owner had come there to see Krissh in person. He let know who he was to the people there and Krissh also made a speech and started the party.

I bought myself a rum this time. It was so cold so I thought something heat is good for the body.
Krissh wanted to dance with Isabelle, So he was busy dancing.

Andrea was chatting with Rahasya.
I went and sat near a cliff and started to drink.
Andrea saw me and she told Rahasya.
Andrea and Rahasya came and sat with me.
Why are you drinking so much Rahul, Andrea asked?
You were not an addict in New Zealand. In fact, you haven't even touched drinks for 3 years. You were so busy yourself and so silent, Why have you become like this, she asked me?
I saw Andrea and smiled.

By the way, Rahul, Rahasya, What happened between you guys, she asked?
I was drunk by that time. I was conscious of what I was speaking but I had no control.

She broke up with me Andrea, I loved her with all my heart, I still do love her and I had so many plans for her. She went away from Australia after knowing that I was in love with her. She was the one who lost the memory, Did I tell her to lose her memory? no, then why did she leave me, I asked?

I stood up and those two also stood up. Andrea was telling Rahul don't make a mess now, We are in the middle of a party.

I hugged Rahasya and started to cry. I thought it was Andrea.

I love her so much Andrea. I wish she's mine forever, I will look after her and live a happy life, Andrea, I said.

She hugged me back. She didn't utter a word. I lost conscious.

I woke up the next day and the first person I saw was Isabelle shouting at Krissh regarding me getting drunk.

I sat and I was in Rahaysa 's room. Rahasya was sitting next to me and was staring at me.

She smiled at me. I was having a very bad headache.

Rahasya gave me a towel and she asked me to get fresh soon.

Isabelle, Don't fight with Krissh, Rahul will not drink and that responsibility is mine, she said.

I finished my shower and I came out.

Rahasya saw me.

I'll wait downstairs, Finish dressing and come down for breakfast, she said. I was confused and didn't know her behavior.

I went down and everybody was waiting for me.
Ah! there you are, Krissh said.
Let's eat, Am hungry, he said.
Rahasya sat beside me and Andrea beside Rahasya.
Rahasya served me.
Krissh was speaking with somebody.
He came and announced everybody, Change of plans amigos.
Have your breakfast and then we are leaving for the Greater Himalayas or Himadri especially to see Mount Everest. The tallest peak in the world, he said.

Are you serious, Isabelle asked sarcastically?
We ain't going to climb the mountain till the peak dumbo, he said.
She looked sarcastically. Oh come on babe, Finish soon and be ready, I'll be outside waiting, he said.
I finished my breakfast and got up. Rahasya was with me.

Andrea was yelling, Wait, Rahul, am still having.
How can you leave your best friend idiot, she asked?
I smiled at her, Alright finish soon, Let's leave, I said.
After that, We boarded the cars and Rahasya was sitting beside me.

I put on my headphones, opened the window and started listening to music without talking to anybody. Isabelle showed me something with actions. I removed my headphones.
What re, I asked?
Excuse me! We have come to enjoy, not to listen to music and sit simply, she said.
Alright, alright, Sorry, I said.

On the way, I slept without my knowledge and Krissh woke me up at the destination. When I woke up, I saw Rahasya laying on my chest.
I didn't want to disturb her. So I put her aside slowly and she woke up. As soon as she woke up, she looked at me like I killed her entire family.
She said sorry. She moved out.
Andrea was looking at me and teasing.
I don't know what got into Andrea.
Rahul, don't worry, By the time we leave, I promise that Rahasya will be with you back as the old girlfriend, she said.

I smiled at her and got out to see God's creation. I was speechless, It was a priceless moment for me to see the tallest mountain in the world and am just as tiny as an ant.
Isabelle was shouting with joy and there was the Indian army placed at the base.
Rahasya was holding my hand.
Rahul, Can I speak to you for a moment, she asked?
Of course, I said.

Please don't drink, At least for the sake of me, she said.

I looked down, she lifted my chin and asked again.

Alright Ammu, as you say, I said.

Rahasya started to enjoy moments with me.

We went through the cable rope up the lower heights and we had snacks together.

Rahasya was telling about her days how she spent in India after she came from Australia.

Andrea was listening to this and smiling. Krissh put me a thumbs up too.

We planned to stay there for the night. The hotel view was a beauty of heaven. We could see the mount beautifully. As the sun moves, It's ray falls on the peak and it looks like a chocolate milkshake with Oreo toppings on the vanilla cream.

We went shopping in the region. I invest money on food more than purchasing things.

There was a lame joke which I always say to Ammu.

"Where's all your money?

Ah! it's safely deposited in my stomach in the form of food."

Isabelle is a shopping addict, we call her shopaholic.

Andrea was confused on what to purchase, she loves Indian things and clothes but she didn't have much of an idea, so Rahasya offered help and sorted out things.

I was sitting in one place and eating pastries. Rahasya and Isabelle came after shopping. They had loads of bags.

You are no use to us, Andrea said.

Am enjoying my dessert, I said.

Oh come on Rahul, Help us with the bags, Rahasya said.

Alright Ammu, I said and took her bags.

Arrey! you help her as soon as Rahasya say, but you don't help me, she said.

I laughed at her and also took her bunch of bags.

You are crazy Andrea, I said.

Later, we went to our rooms and started to pack these things.

I was standing at the hall window view outside of the room and watching the sunset and I wish I had more than two eyes to see such beauty. suddenly as I was enjoying the moment, someone hugged me from behind.

Andrea, come on, leave me and see this beauty of nature, I said.

There were no words from her. She hugged me even tighter. I released myself from her and turned back to see Rahasya crying.

Am sorry Rahul, I know what I did was a mistake. Please forgive me, she said.

She was down on her knees crying at me and asking for forgiveness.

I know I shouldn't have left you that day, It was all my fault, she said.

I stood there watching her.

She cried continuously, I left her and went back to
my room.
I don't know what got into me. The next day I woke
up and spoke to Krissh.
Krissh, Let's go home.
What happened to you brother, he asked?
Am sorry Krissh for spoiling this trip. Either you let
me go or you come with me to Bangalore and I'll
leave the country immediately, I said.

Slow down buddy, tell me what's wrong, he asked?
Please, am not in a mood to tell anything, I said.

He started to convince me, I was not in the mood to
listen to him. I took a bus to Delhi and booked an
emergency flight to New Zealand. I was getting
continuous calls from Rahasya and Krissh. Andrea
didn't come with me.
I left for New Zealand.

(33)

I landed in New Zealand. I left all my luggage back in India. I went to my home opened the door and straight away sat on the couch.
What the hell did I just do, I asked myself?
I couldn't do anything, I was totally confused. I went to my room and slept.

I woke up in the middle of the night. Krissh had called me.
What's wrong with you idiot, he asked?
Why did you just run away like that, he asked?
Sorry Krissh, I was not in the mood.
Where are you right now, he asked?
Am at home, I said.
The connection got cut.

I went for a drive in the middle of the night.
A cop stopped me to check if I was drunk.
I stopped near MCD and went to have a snack.
I sat there, Ordered and had my dinner.
I came back to my car and slept inside the car.

After that, I wanted to become normal so I went back to work. After work, I went to the studio and started speaking ON AIR.
The next day I got an offer from the New Zealand film industry. They asked me to send a voice note of mine and also a small clip of my acting or direction.

I spoke to the director and sent him a small clip of my acting.

After a day, a letter arrived from the Central board of New Zealand film certified.
I was accepted as an artist for the Hollywood. They also selected me for an action movie and asked me to attend the auditions at the Hollywood in Los Angeles.
I was so happy to see my name in the international film industry certification.

I kept it aside. I was so disappointed with my life and I started to work and go to the gym to reduce my stress.
A week just got over like that, It was Sunday and I was at home sitting on my couch watching tv.
I ordered lunch and was waiting for the delivery executive to arrive.

There was a cricket match going on between New Zealand and India.
The match was scheduled at Eden Park in Auckland.
Somebody was knocking at the door.
I thought it was the delivery executive and opened the door.

Krissh, Isabelle, Andrea, Rahasya and my parents were standing at the front of the door.

I didn't know what to react. Come in, I said.
They all came in.

Please sit down.

I went into the kitchen. Isabelle and Rahasya came back of me. I was preparing tea.

What should I do, Isabelle asked?

help me with the cooking, I said.

Immediately I ordered vegetables and all the groceries. I gave tea to parents and others. Lunch came, I kept that in the fridge. Groceries came, I took that and gave it to Isabelle.

Father was watching the news. Mother came running toward the kitchen. She hugged me.

How are you, she asked?

You are living in such a big city, It's so nice here, big house, you are maintaining good, she said.

Krissh came inside. Rahul, After lunch, `we need to discuss with you, he said.

I looked at him. He shook his head and gave me a sign intimating not to worry.

Isabelle and Rahasya helped me out with the cooking.

I served lunch, Everyone was happy with the cooking.

The only person smiling during lunch was my mother.

Krissh, Let's go up. There's a balcony up there big enough for the family, I said.

Sure, It's your call, he said.

Everybody had their lunch, Krissh asked everybody to go up.

I sat on the beanbag. Parents were sitting on the couch.

Krissh started, Rahul, First, I want to tell that I have told everything to your parents, They know everything about Rahasya, he said.

I want to know, what happened at the hotel, Why did you run away, he asked?

It's nothing bro, I said.

Appa started, Rahul, First of all, what you did was wrong, he said.

But, I like her, she's very good and she's the right one for the family. What more is your problem, he asked?

What is your opinion aunty, krissh asked?

She looks like the goddess Lakshmi itself. Am happy with her, she said.

So............... he gave a long pause.

Andrea was looking at my face. Everybody was curious about what I was gonna answer.

I need time appa, I said.

Why, what's wrong, he asked?

Appa, you don't understand, I said.

Alright, give me some time with her, I'll take her out and I want to speak with her alone, I said.

Rahasya lifted her head up. I don't know where that courage came from. Let's go now, she said in excitement.

Andrea looked at me and shook her head.

Alright then, Isabelle, get started for dinner. Rahul will be out for some time, he said.

Rahasya changed her dress, I came out with my same attire what I wore at home.

Outside there were Shridhar and other bodyguards who were guarding the house and the neighbors were looking at me as if the president of united states have arrived at my house.

(34)

I took my car and Krissh called me from up and threw his Ferrari car keys.
Drive safe and enjoy your day, he said. I was smiling at him.

She sat and I started driving. I went 15 blocks away.
Do you want to hang out in the city or the countryside, I asked her?
She was looking out the window and didn't answer me. She was thinking something.

Ammu, I said.
Ya, sorry, what were you telling, she asked?
It's nothing, I said.
I took her to an ice cream parlor and bought her an ice cream and then went to the countryside. It was cold, a bit sunny, silent and peaceful.
We stopped by the Lake Pupuke. Its a heart shaped lake in Auckland.

I went by the pathway which was constructed in the midway lake and sat in the corner.
Rahasya came and sat beside me.

Rahul, Am sorry, It's my fault. I accept that. Please forgive me, she said.
I didn't speak anything, I was looking straight ahead where a kid was playing ashore.
I love you, Rahul, Please give me one more chance, she said.

The kid who was playing fell in the water and he was drowning. He couldn't even shout for help.

Immediately, I jumped in the water and swam across the lake and saved him. He drank a lot of water, so I performed CPR and finally saved him.

His mother was crying. I convinced her and asked her to admit him to a hospital for further problems. I smiled at him and came back.
I was completely wet. The water was freezing.

Sorry, I had to go, I said.
It's okay Rahul, she said.
Rahasya, can I ask you something, I asked?
Of course, Rahul.
Do you remember anything before the accident, I asked?
She put her head down and kept silent.
Tell me, I said.

Rahul, I'll be honest,
I don't remember anything before the accident, I don't even remember you. Whatever I had the memories before the accident is better to forget and leave it to the past. I fell in love with you again and I want to start a new life. I think this is a new beginning in my life.
I'll start it fresh, she said.
But Am very sorry for hurting you and behaving with you like that, I should have never left you, Am very sorry Rahul, she said.

I looked at her and she was never changed. She was the same old beautiful angel. The more I saw her, the more I fell in love with her.
I don't know what happened to me, I kissed her on the lips and hugged her. I started to cry.

She was surprised to see me making such a move.
She smiled at me and hugged me back. She wiped my tears.

Don't cry now, she said.
Let's sit here for a while. I loved this place, she said.
Okay, let's sit. but Am actually freezing, I said.
It's okay sit, a little bit of freezing won't kill you, she said and laughed.
I looked at her and smiled. She was enjoying the view, I was looking at her. I couldn't take my eyes off her.

We came back home, Krissh was sleeping.
Isabelle was busy preparing for dinner. Mother and Andrea were helping her. Father was watching tv.
I went inside. I whispered Rahasya to go to the kitchen.
So, My father paused.
I looked at him. Everything went fine appa, Let Krissh wake up, I'll tell you, I said.
He smiled at me.

I went into the kitchen. What's for dinner, I asked Isabelle.
She looked at me.

Arrey! Krissh is sleeping like a boar. And am preparing here taking the help of amma and Andrea, she said.
Alright, Alright, Do you want another set of hands, I asked her?

Nope, you araamse sit down, I'll handle this, Rahasya, help me re. Let the kings sit down and rest, she said.
Did you eat something Rahasya, she asked.
Yeah! sis, Rahul bought me lunch, she said.

After a few minutes, Krissh woke up.
Arrey! so soon you came back huh, he asked?
Krissh, check out the time, I said.
Oh damn! It's already snack time, Good evening everyone, he said.
Rahasya smiled at Krissh and she showed thumbs up to him.
Krissh didn't want to eat lunch, As it was evening, he said he will have tea. and later for dinner let's have lunch.

We were sitting on the balcony and having tea.
father was speaking about his childhood days.
Suddenly Krissh said, What about Rahul's marriage appa.
Rahasya was shy, she put her head down.

Rahul started acting like he got a phone call, In fact, he really got a phone call from Hollywood. They asked him to attend the auditions coming the weekend and they also arranged tickets for his journey.

He was very happy to hear this. Attending the auditions in Hollywood is a dream come true.

Well, before that, I want to know something between you guys, he said.

Are you happy to marry my son Mohle, he asked in Malayalam?

With a shy, she shook her head telling yes.

What about you Rahul, he asked?

Am ready appa, I love her too, I said.

Well, that's settled, Krissh, Am going to fix the engagement this coming month after he attends the auditions, appa said.

Definitely appa, I'll arrange everything for that.

Anyway, Rahasya, as he's going to attend the auditions, why don't you go with him to the United States, After all, it's going to be a trip and also you will be visiting Hollywood, he said?

Don't worry about amma, I'll take care and arrange everything by the time you come back, he said.

Even I'll go, Isabelle said. Seeing this even Andrea said that she too will join.

Why Isabelle, Krissh asked?

Pleaasssseeeeee, Isabelle pleaded.

Alright, you guys can also join, But I'll be sending the bodyguards with you guys, he said.

"No Problemo," Isabelle said.

Krissh booked the same flight in which we were going.

We stayed the rest of the week. Later that weekend we flew to Los Angeles, United States.

They went back to India for the arrangements.

<u>ACT 10: Los Angeles, the United States</u>

(35)

Welcome to Los Angeles, airport staff said.

They greeted us with a namaste gesture. It was wonderful t see that the Indian style is been used on the western side.

We found two to three Indian families at the airport. one of their children recognized Isabelle. They were funny and crazy. They took selfies with us.

We came out and there was a Hollywood bus waiting in front of the airport. People were trying to peep inside the Hollywood caravan. Media had surrounded the caravan.

A guy was waiting at the entrance with a name board written on it, Rahul.

I raised my hand and the bodyguards were offered to us. Our own men had also surrounded us. It was like protecting the president of united states.

People gathered around us, Some were taking pictures of us and then immediately this guy pushed me into the caravan and the bus started and we left. The caravan was so huge there was everything inside.

Isabelle asked to switch on the news. It was broadcasting live, Rahul from India have come to attend auditions at Hollywood. Rahul is seen at the LAX airport.

Isabelle was laughing.

Arrey! just for attending auditions our Rahul has become a star in the states. This is awesome, Andrea said.

I was totally blank. Rahasya was looking outside the window.

Rahul, People are so crazy they are following the bus, she said

Hello, Welcome to Los Angeles. Sorry for the inconvenience. My name is Mark, the guy with the name board said.

Hello Mark, You don't look like American, Isabelle said.

He laughed, Am not American. Am basically from India, I was born and bought up in the states he said.

Am working in Hollywood from the production team. The authorities sent me because they thought that you guys will be comfortable with an Indian. But am surprised to see that your friends are foreigners, he said.

Isabelle laughed, Well Mark, Am married to an Indian and settled in India. We were first in Australia, Now Rahul is settled in New Zealand, Isabelle said.

Mam, I have seen you somewhere, Your face is a lot familiar, Mark said.

Andrea smiled, Do you know Krissh from India, she asked?

Of course, Who doesn't know. He's world famous, Mark said.

Well, Actually Isabelle is the wife of Krissh, she said.

Mark stood up in excitement and he couldn't believe his eyes. He asked for a selfie, and we all took photos of him too.

Well mam, Until you leave the states, the responsibility is mine to take care. Ask me anything, I'll arrange here anything for you guys, he said.

That's so kind of you Mark, Andrea said.

We reached Hollywood, he said.

We got down, A warm welcome was given by the Hollywood staffs. Mark arranged rooms for us to stay inside the Hollywood. We freshened up and that following day, we went for a shopping outside.

Mark arranged dinner and the whole day was enjoyed. The next day was the auditions.

We slept earlier that night as Rahul should wake up with a fresh mind.

(36)

The next day we woke up, I was awake and was practicing. Those guys were recording my activities. It was funny.
Later everybody was ready to see my auditions. I was damn scared. My pulse rate was increasing every time I think of the auditions.

Mark helped me to ease down. He said that even if you get rejected don't worry. As you have attended the Hollywood auditions, It will broadcast on tv and 90% of the people are famous because of the broadcasting. Attending the Hollywood auditions are like rock stars. I met so many celebrities over the waiting hall.

Those three girls were together and they were watching me. Rahasya was smiling and telling me not to worry.
One by one people were going in and most of them came out with crying faces.
I was confused that these guys were crying because they got rejected or selected.
The hall was huge, It had big boom speakers, A very huge stage where the directors and the producers were sitting together and watching the auditions.

Suddenly, they announced, next Rahul from India.
I stood up, Isabelle was whispering all the best. I went straight ahead.

Hello Mr. Rahul.

Can you introduce yourself, a person with a blonde beard who looked like a janitor was sitting on a chair, asked me?

Hello America! I started.

People from back started to shout with excitement, They were so happy listening to an Indian saying the words America.

Am Rahul. Am basically from India. But settled in New Zealand.

Am an RJ (radio jockey) in New Zealand. I love acting, painting, I love to entertain people. One of my dreams is to act in an action movie, I said.

Well alright Rahul, show me what do you got? spill that talent and spread among us, he said.

I was so scared, slowly I started to act, I started to show the stunts.

He said, stop!

I stopped and everybody stood up. I thought that was the worst performance and am rejected.

He stayed silent for a few minutes. Nobody spoke a word.

I stayed there and didn't move to see what was his reply.

Suddenly he replied, Being an Indian, coming here to Hollywood and attending the auditions is great. In that getting selected for a global release movie given as a villain role is just a miracle, he said.

Everybody started to shout. The whole show was broadcasted on Indian televisions and I was the first

Indian to get selected in Hollywood even before making a movie in India.

Born and bought up in a small town and getting fame in a single day was like something which God came down and showered the blessings. I couldn't believe my eyes.
Isabelle and Rahasya were crying with happiness.

I never expected this to happen. Finally, the director came towards me and he hugged me. Welcome to Hollywood Rahul, he said.
We celebrated that day and he invited me and my friends to a party.

(37)

The next day was the agreement session and discussion.
my enrollment was the last for the whole set but even they never expected that an Indian will get selected.

As per the agreement they had placed me that I will be working for the movie as a villian role and I will be paid a total amount of 1500$ Crores and will get the 30% of the share after the movie gets a share collection globally.
I was surprised to see my pay. It all happened suddenly. I signed the agreement and then we invited the director for our marriage. Of course, It was a verbal invitation. We spoke to Mark and invited him too. We gave him some amount of money. He didn't accept, but Isabelle convinced telling that you are like my brother. Take this money from sister. He was happy.

We packed up back to India and the traveling expense was given by the Hollywood. It was nice of them. Mark dropped us to the airport in the Hollywood caravan and even he provided security guards to escort us.
We soon reached back to India.

ACT 11: My father

(38)

We reached India, I got a call from Krissh as soon as I landed.

Hey buddy! We just landed, I said
Rahul, book a taxi and come to Vikram hospital.
Why, what happened, are you alright, I asked?
Just come, I'll tell you later.
He hung up the phone.

I was scared.
What is it, Isabelle asked me?
I don't know, Krissh just asked us to book a taxi and go to Vikram hospital now, I said.
Where's he?
He's at the hospital, that's what he said me.
Okay chill, Let's go, hurry up, she said.

We booked a taxi and asked him to take us to the Vikram hospital.

We reached.
Krissh was waiting at the entrance.
I got down.

What's the matter buddy?
He eyeballed Isabelle and she ran straight.
Don't worry, he said.
Tell me what's wrong, I said.

He started to sweat.
I'll tell you but please calm down.
It's your father, he had a heart attack, he said.
I started to shake.

I ran upstairs and he took me to ICU.
I went there and I could see my father just lying on the bed.
All my dreams just became dust by just seeing him in that condition.

My mom and brother were sitting outside the ICU.
Amma was crying badly and brother was convincing her.
Rahasya seeing all this, she sat at one place with tears.
Isabelle was with Krissh holding hands together
Rahasya's amma started to hug her and cry,
I was speechless.
Doctor came. Who is the relative of Mr. Chandran, he asked?

I stood up. You are, he asked?
Am the son of the patient, I said.
Well, Can I speak to you I private, he said.

Krissh came with me.
Patient has a block in his heart and he have 90% chances to have another heart attack.
But I can help to avoid that by performing a surgery, he said.
I need to put a stunt and clear the blockage, he said.

Do whatever it takes to save him doctor, I'll arrange everything for that, Krissh said.
Two bodyguards were standing behind Krissh.
And you are, the doctor asked?

Am Krissh doctor.
You're the actor right, he asked?
The very same doctor, he said.
Doctor started to sweat and he started to stutter.
Don't worry Krissh, I will definitely save him, he said.

I'll start the operation once his blood pressure is down. The BP is fluctuating sir, he said.

I'll arrange everything for the operation, Krissh said.
I hugged Krissh and cried very badly.
Don't worry brother. Am always with you, he said.
Midnight was the operation.

We were waiting outside the operation theatre.
Nobody had dinner. I asked to go have dinner.
I don't want, Rahul, Am not hungry, she said.
I looked at Krissh and asked him to convince.

Amma, go have dinner, It's okay, I'll take care, he said.
Isabelle go with her, he said.
Rahasya you too, I said.
She nodded her head and they went to have dinner from the hospital canteen.

The doctor came out after the surgery. It was 12:30 midnight.

After the surgery, the doctor came out.
It went successfully.
Mr. Krissh came at the right time or else we would have lost him, he said.
Well, I need him in observation, after 2 days he can be discharged, he said.

You can purchase these tablets in the pharmacy and I need somebody to take extra care regarding him. Everyday morning and night after breakfast and dinner this tablet should be consumed, he said.

I'll take care of that, Krissh said.
Krissh, I want to speak with you, I said.
Isabelle, Andrea, and my mom came.

Amma, the doctor said he's fine. Surgery's been successful, I said.
He has prescribed some medicines and he should consume that every day. He can be discharged after 2 days, I said.
Can I see him now, she asked?
One sister was standing near the OT. We will be shifting him to the ward. He should rest, Please don't speak to him for a while, she said.

They shifted him and I can see stitches on his chest.
He was in deep sleep.
Amma was sitting beside him resting her head on the bed.

Andrea and Isabelle with Rahasya were sitting out.

Krissh came out.
Yes, What was it that you want to speak to me, he asked?
Krissh, It's that. I can't leave him in this condition and can marry Rahasya, I said.
It's okay Rahul, Why are you worrying?
It's the matter of few days. He will be alright Rahul, he said.
No, Krissh, am not satisfied leaving him like this. Let me handle this, I said.
Well, Alright. Am not going to force you regarding this.
Once he recovers, then we will arrange all your things, he said.
But how am going to tell this to Rahasya?
Don't worry, I'll speak to her, he said.

He spoke to Rahasya regarding this in the hospital ward. She seemed okay with Krissh's decisions.
She said okay.
I spent day and night in the hospital. I didn't move from his side.
After three days, the doctor asked us to discharge him and he's completely fine.

Krissh arranged transport and we came home.
As soon as we reached, Appa said. " alright, let's arrange my son's marriage."
I looked at him.
Appa, I think We will keep this marriage for later.
First, I want you to recover, I said.

What nonsense are you telling? we can't postpone
your marriage, It's the big day of your's, he said.
No appa, First, you come inside. We will speak to
you regarding this.
Krissh came and convinced appa to take him in.

Isabelle, get a glass of water.
Then make him tea, he said.
Appa drank the water.
now tell me, why you guys want to postpone my
son's marriage?
Uncle, You are like my father. Now imagine this is
my marriage. When you are in this condition, how
can I leave you and get married?
I can't leave my father like this. Once you recover,
we will start the arrangements, Krissh said.

Where is my son? call him.
Ha, appa, tell me, I said.
Call your mother also, he said.
Kamakshi, Please tell him that not to stop the
marriage, he pleaded.
It's my one last wish, he said.
Hearing this Rahasya was in tears and she fell at his
feet.
Please appa, don't tell like that. You have so many
more dreams. Don't tell this is your last wish.
My eyes filled with tears.
Appa you take rest. We will talk about this later, I
said.

Everybody left the room and he slept.
The rumors hit the media.

Some said that my father died.
I called the media.

Everybody was in front of the house.
Questions were asked continuously.
Krissh came.
He did a namaskar.
When people were starting to ask questions, he raised his hand to stop.
Am here to announce something.
" I heard that were rumors hitting the social media and even you guys telling that the marriage has been canceled due to the death of Rahul's father."
Well, the part where his father expired is completely false.
His father is still alive and again, the marriage is not been canceled. It has been just postponed. he said.
Please, don't make false statements in the name of this. Thank you, ladies and gentlemen.
Please leave quietly. He's resting, he said.

They all left and that was broadcasted day and night.
I saw people trolling Krissh in social media. But they troll him in a good way.

I took personal initiative in the matter of my father.
Krissh had offered a doctor and a nurse at home but still I was scared.

(39)

After 6 months...............

Everything was fine.
Krissh and I went to the invitation printing center and we spoke to them.
We were happy and the next day It was the invitation printing and distributing ceremony.
It was a happy day.
Amma was very busy in the kitchen and appa was involved in cooking too.
He tied a towel around his head like a chef.
I was very happy to see everybody working.

I was on the terrace. I sat down and started to think about the marriage.
Krissh's house is huge. Totally three buildings with helipad and stuff. So I was sitting and there is a window which is visible from the second building and It's clearly visible what I do.
Rahasya has seen me.
She climbed the ladder slowly and came.
What are you doing here when the whole world is working for our marriage?
nothing, Rahasya. I was thinking about how my father bought me up and then we stopped talking and now all of a sudden we are speaking but I regret the days I haven't spoken to him.
It's okay Rahul.
Why are you worrying about him?

He's the happiest face, I've seen today among the people, she said.

Yeah! You are right. I've got nothing to worry.
I started to touch her hair.
She closed her eyes.
Slowly, I went near and kissed her.
Andrea was looking from the window.
Wow, I think the first night is getting finished before the marriage amigo, she shouted from the window.
Rahasya was shy, she ran downstairs.
I looked at Andrea.
She was laughing continuously.

It was dinner time.
All my relatives were there.
children's were running around.
Krissh's dining table is a huge one. Twenty to twenty-two people can sit and eat all together.
Everybody was sitting and the dinner was served.
Appa was having the dinner happily.
Across the table, Isabelle and Krissh, Andrea and children's, Amma with appa, relatives, People were enjoying the dinner.
After dinner, we were sitting outside to rest.
As we spoke, Appa said.
"Dear Rahul, I want to see my grandson soon. I hope I live till that. I've aged up. I'll be going soon."
how many times I have told you not to speak like that, I said.
Come on appa, Don't speak like that. It hurts, Krissh said.

Alright, alright. I was just kidding. Come on cheer up. Don't be with the long face appa told.

We all went to sleep.
in the mid of the night, I heard a sound. I woke up to check it out.
Dogs were barking. I went out and the guards said It's nothing.
Rahasya stayed with us but I never slept with her. She used to sleep with Andrea near to my room.
Andrea always checks appa in the middle of the night.
That particular night amma had slept with Andrea and Rahasya.

The next day It was Invitation distribution ceremony. Appa used to wake up early but he was asleep.
It was 08:00 in the morning and he still didn't wake up.
I went to check appa to get him ready.
Appa, wake up, It's late already.
Appa, Wake up, I'll get the tea ready, I said.
I had some papers in my hand so I was concentrating on that and waking appa.
Finally, I kept those documents aside and woke him up. He was frozen like stone.
He was cold.
He was no more.
I started to cry aloud, I called Krissh.
People came running. Immediately ambulance was arranged and he was taken to the hospital.

The doctor tried in every way. He shook his head and said sorry to Krissh.

Amma ran inside the ward, Krissh's eyes were filled with tears.

Andrea was inside confused and crying.

my mother was crying so badly and Isabelle was convincing her.

Rahasya sat down on her knees and started to cry so badly.

Krissh sat down on the chair.

The doctor came.

"Am really sorry sir, I've tried to bring back the patient to life. But according to me, the patient has died in his sleep."

Hospital declared brought dead and the death certificate was produced.

I was confused, I didn't know what to do.

My parents were the reason I grew up like a king.

"When I was a kid, I said to my father that one day we will be rich, we had nothing, that day appa said, we won't become rich in this life Rahul, but now I have everything but I don't have my father."

We brought the body back to home.

Media people were present there. Krissh didn't do anything.

Relatives and friends came to visit him for one last time.

My mother was crying badly. Of course, she knows him better than anyone in this world.

I sat down and did nothing but see his face.

I had no strength in me.

Krissh went out to media. Please don't ask anybody questions. Today we lost Rahul's father.
That's all I have to say.
Media understood and they didn't disturb us.
Police had surrounded us and they were controlling the usual crowd.

One by one everybody came and paid their respect.
We kept the body for a day and then we needed to do all the karmas.
The next day we arranged a hearse van from home to the graveyard. We don't bury the bodies, we burn them.
So the arrangements for that also was made.
I made all the puja and then we took the body.
My mother shouldn't come to the graveyard. No ladies are allowed to the graveyard as it is followed in the culture.
I was the person who handled all the Karma being the first son of the family.

Krissh was with me the entire time. Some relatives spent volunteered and helped us with all the stuff.
Amma saw him for the last time and we shifted the body to the hearse van.
Amma started to cry loudly. It was painful to see her like that.
We reached the cemetery. We kept the body on the Fireplace.
Wood and sticks were kept on the body. The cemetery in charge came.

Shall I close the face? Once I close the face it shouldn't be opened according to the culture, he said.

Krissh looked at me.

I cried literally.

Please wait, I want to see my father for one last time.

I put a ring which was his given by his father. He once said that "even if I die, I should die with this ring on my finger." So I put the ring and kissed on his forehead.

I closed the face.

They gave me a wood which was lit on fire.

Krissh poured ghee all over the body and the wood so it gets burned soon.

I lit the body on fire.

It started to burn.

One by one the bones started breaking. I could hear the noise.

I just stood there and remembered all the words of his.

It was the most painful day of my life.

He was alive yesterday and today he's no more.

Until yesterday we called him by his name but today he's become a body. How soon the time just flew, I love you appa, I said.

Krissh came near and hugged me.

It's okay Rahul. Am there for you, he said.

The body was completely burnt after an hour.

We took the ashes and put it into a box.

The same day, all karmas and puja were done at home and I left to Kerala to dispose of his ashes in the river.
Krissh was with me the entire time.
I prepared balls of rice for the crow's and then that was offered to the crows.
Finally, after everything, I disposed of the ashes.
It was over.

(40)

I came back to Bangalore.
Amma became lonely. She stopped doing all the work.
She stopped eating, drinking.
I convinced her to have food.
The marriage was canceled for now. There were no plans.

Rahasya looked at me.
Rahul, I'll go back to my home. Everything will be okay. I'll be in touch with you, she said.
She hugged me.
Krissh arranged a car and they went back.
Relatives went back to their home.
Messages were piled up in my mobile and lot of emails were unattended.

2 months passed, I was in Krissh's house.
He offered me and my family shelter, food and everything which is in need.
Amma was insisting me to take her back to Kerala.
I arranged one old lady to take care of the house which was in Kerala.
The construction of the new house was completed by 80%
I wanted to get that finished. So I left to Kerala and resumed all the work of the house.
First thing I wanted to do was get the house inaugurated and then shift my mom to the new house.

The house my parents lived should be sold and give all the money to my mom.

I went back to Kerala and resumed all the work.
The house was constructed and it was all ready within a month.
I fixed a date for house warming ceremony.
I Invited everybody.
Everybody came and the house was lit with lights and it was a happy moment but I wished my father was present. He always wanted to live in that new home.
Rahasya came.
How are you?
Am good, Rahul.
How about you?
Am good. How's the house?
It's wonderful.
How's amma? Is she okay now?
Yeah! she misses dad. But she's happy.
Krissh came.
Hey buddy, he said and hugged me.
Well, congratulations! The house is well built.
Thank you Krissh, I said.

Krissh went straight to amma.
He fell at her feet.
Amma, I need to speak with you regarding Krissh and Rahasya. Time is flying, I said.
Rahasya came.
Amma, I'll stay here tonight.
Krissh, stay back, I want to speak something regarding uncle, she said.

What about him, Amma asked?
This is not the right time, amma, she said.

Evening everybody left.
It was a memorable day.
After dinner, Rahasya asked us to gather in the living room.

Rahul, The day Uncle expired, I was with him. I heard a noise and woke up in the middle of the night.
I went to Uncle's room and he was sweating continuously.
He asked me a glass of water. Before I left the room. He caught my hand.
"Rahasya, get married to my son, I think it's time for me to go. I have one last wish. Please get married to Rahul and don't ditch him in the middle. I love you like my own daughter," he said.
When he said that I didn't take it seriously. He drank the glass of water and slept. The next day.......... she paused.
I was surprised.
Amma got up from her place. She hugged Rahasya.
Dear one, you are the light of this house.
Krissh, arrange everything for my son's marriage.
First thing in my list is my son's marriage, she said.
Yes, amma, I'll handle it, he said.

Rahasya fell at her feet.
God bless you, my dear, she said.

Krissh went and met a pujari and the date of my marriage was fixed.
He arranged everything for the marriage.

ACT 11: The Grand finale

Marriage, that's how it went...

(41)

We reached India.
Krissh and my parents were at his home. He arranged a car to bring Rahasya's parents from Kerala. He had arranged everything for the marriage. As soon as we came, he asked us to freshen up.
The next day Krissh conducted Invitation ceremony with Pooja.

Only a few people were present and it was a small ceremony. His family members and ours were present for the invitation ceremony.
After the pooja, I handed the invitation first to my parents and their parents. We fell at their feet and took blessings.
It was a happy moment.

I asked Rahaysa to take one invitation and frame it as a souvenir for the rest of our life. She was smiling.
Later the marriage date was fixed. I was so scared.
That day I went straight to the room and stood in front of the mirror. I was talking to myself.

"Rahul, This is your life, This is the moment. Don't be scared. You have waited for this moment from the day you saw Rahasya.
It will all go right, just stay calm Rahul"
Rahasya entered the room.
What are you doing here, she asked?
I was stuttering with words.

Come downstairs Rahul People are waiting for you, she said.

Before she left, I called her.
Rahasya!
She turned back, What is it Rahul, she asked?
You will not leave me again right, I asked her with a low tone voice filled with fear.

She smiled at her, she gave me a kiss on my forehead and said, Rahul, no matter what, I will lead the life with you with sickness and happiness until my last breath.
I was literally crying.
she hugged me and then I was ready.

The invitations were distributed personally, Through posts, I sent one invitation for William's too.
Andrea was with me all the time helping me with all the arrangements.

I invited everybody in my family.
Totally 1500 invitations were distributed personally and the invitation was put in newspapers and social

media welcoming an open invitation for the people from Krissh's side.

The invitation was also broadcasted through news channels.

It all went well and we came back to Krissh's place. Krissh arranged the palace ground in Bangalore for the reception and the marriage was set in Kerala.

Buses were arranged from Bangalore to Kerala for the people to attend the marriage.

Once we reached Kerala, People were busy with all their stuff.

Everybody was busy including Andrea and Rahasya.

The marriage was conducted 9 km away from our house. so we stayed there that night.

I sat in my room totally confused. I was in a situation where I couldn't tell myself that whether I was happy or sad.

I was shivering with excitement.

Next day, It was my marriage. I went to meet Rahasya and all the ladies were surrounded her.

One girl stood up.

Hey Rahul buddy, please leave Rahasya alone for one day. From tomorrow she's yours forever. We need her tonight, she said.

Andrea was sitting there.

All the ladies pushed me out and locked the door.

Andrea came out.

Anything emergency Rahul, she asked me?

Nothing Andrea, I was feeling alone, I said.
She's feeling scared Rahul, So we are there for her to convince her, she said.
Alright, take care of her, I said.

It was 11:00 pm and I had no sleep.
Everyone was awake.
Krissh came.
Arrey, Rahul! You didn't sleep huh, he asked?
I smiled at him.
I can understand your situation. but this is your day buddy.
It will go alright. Am with you, stay happy, he said.
His words eased me a bit.

I dropped a message to Rahasya. She didn't reply.
I called Isabelle. It was 1:00 a.m.
Ayoo Rahul, you didn't sleep, she asked?
It's 1:00 a.m buddy, go sleep, today is your big day, she said.
What are you doing Isabelle, I asked?
Am having dinner Rahul, she said.
It's so late, I asked?
I know Rahul, I was so busy with all your stuff, I forgot to have dinner.
Thank you so much for this Isabelle. You are sacrificing a lot for me, I said.
It's nothing, Shhhhhhhhhh! be quiet, Don't tell like that. You are my close friend.
Now go sleep, It's late. I'll see you tomorrow, she said and hung the phone.

(42)

Early morning at 4:00 everybody got up an started the arrangements. As I slept late I was damn tired. I slept and when people woke me, I told them that I'll get up at 5:30.
I woke up at 6:00. I came out and everybody was ready and they were staring at me as if I had murdered the whole family.
Andrea came, Rahul, Go on she pushed me inside the bathroom and asked me to get ready soon.

I was ready and the Muhurtham timings were at 08:30 in the morning.
People were in such a hurry, I felt like I was not the one who's getting married.
My father was with uncle gangs, It was funny how all the men and ladies go separate ways ina ceremony.
I was searching for Rahasya. I didn't see her anywhere.
Krissh was with me.

My father's and mother's side relatives, Rahasya's relatives, everybody was at the buses. I didn't know how they were related to me.

Buses took off to the wedding hall.
We came in the car.
We reached the wedding hall.
There were media, Our marriage was showing live in tv channels.

Krissh with some of my friends and some children's accompanied me to Kalyana Mandapam (wedding hall)
I sat there and after a few minutes, a group of girls came and Rahasya came behind.

She wore a grand red saree covered with golden borders. she was like a goddess. I couldn't take my eyes off her.
Isabelle, Andrea, her mother, and my mother was with her.
She sat beside me. Sitting there in the wedding hall I couldn't believe that am getting married to my love.
There was a huge crowd waiting as well as people outside were started to peep and see us.

It was time, The pujari instructed me to take the Mangalasutra (Thaali)
I took it. He said It's time, Tie the knot. Rahasya was putting her head down with shy.
I tied the knot as she bowed down. I don't know what was wrong with people, but people started clapping and then they started blessing.

Usually, when I attended the marriage nobody used to clap, but this was the first time.

Rahasya looked at me, she whispered.
"Rahul, Finally we are married with a happy wide face."

People all got up and they were asked to have breakfast.
Pujari got up. Live a happy life both of you, he said.
We fell at his feet in the presence of God.

I was so damn hungry.
Rahasya saw me and asked me what's the matter?
Nothing dear, just hungry, I said.
Oh, my baby's hungry, Alright wait let me arrange for us, she said.

Our marriage was finally over. It was that simple.
Rahasya looked at Krissh.
brother, We are hungry. Can we have breakfast or are there any formalities for that, she asked?
No dear, there are no formalities. You guys can have breakfast, he said.
We went and sat in the dining area, We had breakfast.

After breakfast, we had photo sessions. It was a public photo session were a lot of unknown people came and they took autographs of us, selfies with Krissh, It was fun. I arranged a few games so that people can participate there and spend some time with us.
Later people boarded the buses and everybody was sent back.

We both came back in the car. I was so damn tired, I slept like hell with my mouth wide open on the way back.

Rahasya and Andrea took photos of me and they posted online.

"Just married and my hubby's already bored of his life."

The photos were funny though.

We reached home. Rahasya's mother started to cry and eventually, she started to cry.

Amma, I might be taking your lamp to my house, but I'll make sure that she will be happy and in no way she will be hurt.

Even though we are in New Zealand I'll make sure that she calls you every day and the moment we land here, First, we will be heading here, I said.

She hugged me and said, "you are one in a million Rahul."

Krissh clapped and then the others. Whatever I said was broadcasted without my knowledge.

We went to our house. People were still there and we arranged lunch and dinner for that day.

People came home and wished us.

One by one people were presenting gifts and we conducted a photo session.

It was fun.

Andrea and Isabelle were having fun and they started games and entertainment.

Dance programs, Mimicry, songs, Quiz. People were having a good time.

I and Rahasya also joined. Krissh and I started mob flash dance. We danced in the middle and others joined.

(43)

That night after dinner, we packed our stuff to go to Bengaluru.

Everything went well. Finally, everybody boarded the cars and started our journey back.

I don't know what happened to me but I slept like a buffalo till Bengaluru.

Krissh was awake the whole night. Isabelle kept Andrea busy with conversations.

We reached Krissh's house.

Ah! finally, we reached. Now it's going to be a mega blast for Rahul's and Rahasya's wedding reception, Krissh said.

Isabelle looked at Krissh and smiled.

Babe, I'll go and start the work. You start the arrangements for tonight, Isabelle said.

I went upstairs and freshened up.

I came down for a coffee.

Rahasya was busy inside the kitchen with Isabelle and Andrea.

Krissh called up Makeup artists for evening's ceremony.

Lot's of people were trying to peep inside the compound to meet me and Krissh.

I couldn't speak with Rahasya that day. She was running around here and there regarding the clothes and the usual stuff.

The makeup artists arrived. They were thoroughly checked and sent in for me and Rahasya.

Clothes were bought. It was a traditional look, I wore the Manyavar's specially made for me. It was ordered, remodified and arranged by Krissh.

Rahasya's clothes were Anarkali. I couldn't see it as Krissh told me to see her once she gets ready.

Rahasya boarded a car separately. It was a total surprise. I tried to see her and but I didn't have a clear view.

We all boarded the cars and went to the palace ground.

As we reached there I saw a huge crowd screaming Rahul, Rahul, Rahul.......

The crowd was controlled by Bengaluru cops and guards. There were bouncers. Some people started to scream Krissh, Krissh and they wanted to see him. Of course am not famous. People cheer my name because Krissh was the one who organized my marriage and made it a memorable one. Krissh made me famous.

We were guided to the rooms.

Krissh made an entry to the stage and the crowd went mad.

Krissh raised his hands and did a namaskar.

Hello, ladies and gentlemen, I thank all of you who is present here.

This is broadcasting live on every media and channels. Today is the day where my best friend is married to one of the most beautiful women in this world.

Am happy to see here and I wish them a very happy married life.

I want you guys to support us and make this wedding reception go smoothly. People can have dinner and there are varieties of dishes available.
Please don't waste or throw away the food.
And also the food will be delivered to Old age homes and orphanages.

I present you Rahul and Rahasya, Krissh said.
I was so scared, But then I went and there I saw Rahasya coming.
She wore Royal blue half Anarkali and a royal blue blouse. With those lights and the crowd cheering up, I was just looking at her. Media were focusing on me.
That look on Rahul's face definitely defined how well he takes care of his wife, Krissh said.
I smiled. There was a different lane for celebrities.
Different lane for the public and different lane for our relations.

Media people were given some positions and they were focusing from every angle with the zoom lens.
Isabelle and Andrea was with me on stage.
There were two big thrones to sit for us.
The photo session started and one by one celebrity, politicians started coming.

They wished us, blessed us and after a photo one by one left.
We asked everybody to have dinner.
One fellow jumped off the barriers and came straightly to us. So many people pushed him and

they were trying to put him down, he jumped straight to us and guards surrounded us. He started crying.
I asked him to let him go.

Sorry sir for such an embarassing entry, he said.
It's okay, tell me, I said.
I want to take a photo with you and Krissh sir as well as Isabelle mam, he said. He pleaded a lot.

I looked at Krissh and he came. He stood beside that guy and took selfies and also we all stood beside him and took a picture. He was so happy.
Don't miss the dinner amigo, Krissh said.
Thank you, sir, he said and he fell at mine and Krissh's feet.

Hey, don't do that, I said and sent him.

There was a big screen like they set it up in the cricket stadium so that other's can se how all came.
As I was standing I saw William's on the screen. he was sittin g in the VIP section.
I took the mic and announced.

Mr. William's, the one who's sitting in the VIP section.
He looked at me. Isabelle looked at him and asked him to come on stage.
As soon as he came I hugged him. Isabelle and Krissh gave him a warm welcome.
I was happy that he has come to my wedding reception.

We asked him to have dinner.
Isabelle said, William's, after dinner don't leave.
Stay back. He smiled at her and said yes.

Everything went well and I was so happy. My
whole day spent watching her.
My parents were sitting and they were having
dinner. I was hungry and tired. Everybody left and
then we went to have dinner.

Finally, after dinner we went back to Krissh's house
and I don't know what happened. As soon as I
reached the room, I slept in my wedding dress
without knowledge.

I woke up the next day and Rahasya looked at me
with a cup of coffee.
You were so damn tired, you had no time for our
first night, she said.

I smiled at her and pulled her to bed and hugged
her. Let's finish our first night in my home town, I
said.
Kerala again, she asked?
Naaa, New Zealand, I said.
Oh! alright as you wish, she said and she pushed me
inside bathroom to get me freshened up.

I came downstairs to see Isabelle, Krissh, William,
and Andrea sitting together having tea.
Krissh looked at me.
Ah! finally. The king is awake.

You overslept brother, William said.
I was so damn tired brother. It's been a happy rough day standing continously for hours, I said.
I know, anyway have tea, he said.

After a long pause, Krissh looked at me.
So what next, he asked me?
Am married to my dream girl, So I'll be going to New Zealand, have kids, start a family, hollywood offer's and a good time with my family, I said.
So that means you are not coming back to India, he asked me?
Hey no, It's not like that. Of course, my family is settled here.
I can't forget them and after all you guys are family too. So eventually, I'll be coming back here to see you guys, take some responsibilities, and then let my children's play with yours, I said.
Krissh laughed.
Well done buddy, you will lead a happy life, he said.

I turned down to William. What about you buddy, What are you gonna do, no plans of marriage, I asked?
He smiled, Eventually I'll get there, he said.

Well, when are you leaving India, he asked me?
I'll be leaving tomorrow, I said.
So soon! you could have spent some days here and then leave, William asked?
It's that I gotta do some work and the usual stuff, I said.

Alright buddy, all the best. I'll be leaving india tonight.

Hey, There's a send off party today, So attend the party and then leave, krissh said.

The party got started, William enjoyed a bit but didn't want to drink as he's leaving. It was a happy moment in my life. Am finally married and am going to start my life.

It was late, William wanted to leave. Krissh arranged a car for him to drop off at the airport.

Phewww!!! That was a fantastic marriage, I said.

Rahasya looked at me in wonder. Are you serious, she asked?

Why not, It was fun, happy, good food, and we are husband and wife, I said and giggled.

I slept as soon as possible for the next day's flight.

It was morning, I woke up soon. freshed up.

Babe, get up, I said.

five more minutes Rahul, she said.

I went and my things were packed already.

Krissh was awake and he was spending his morning walk in his garden with a cup of coffee.

So you're leaving huh, he asked?

Yeah, buddy! I should go. Don't worry, Am always there with you. I won't forget what you have done for me. You are my guardian angel buddy, I said.

His eyes were filled with tears.

He came forward and hugged me.

I tapped on his back.

Isabelle came with coffee.
Don't forget us, Rahul, she said.
She hugged me.
Have this coffee. let me wake your wife, she said.

It was soon noon.

(44)

Our flight was at 3:00 pm.
Everything was finally ready.
We boarded our cars after lunch.
We reached the airport.
Everybody was present at the airport to bid us goodbye.

Oh! my mom started crying, then her parents started.
Of course, I know the pain. I looked at Rahasya.
She started crying and she ran towards her parents and hugged them.

Isabelle's eyes were filled with tears.
I somehow controlled myself but ended up crying too.
Everybody bid us goodbye one by one. I had some money and I gave it to my mother.
She refused but I insisted to take them.
Mom gave me some homemade pickle.
Ah! my favorite thing.

It was time for us. We took our luggage and went through the security gates.
Rahasya was looking back for one last time before we leave and then we went inside.
We finished all the formalities and then boarded ourselves.
The flight took off. Rahasya held my hand.

I love you, Rahul. We are going to start a new life,
she said.
Yes, baby, we will, we will, I said.

(45)

And that's how I married your mother, I said.
But papa, Did you really fall in love with mummy,
she asked?
Why do you have that doubt baby?
Because her face is painted like hell and all the time
she will be in front of the mirror.
Hahahahahaha! that's funny. Well, Yes of course, I
fell in love with your mother and even now I do and
will be the same forever and ever, I said.
Well, Baby it's time for you to sleep.
Good night, sleep tight, let the bed bugs bite.
Muah! I kissed good night.

Well, babe, she's slept, I said.
Did you convince her?
Of course, I said the entire story.
What story, she asked?
Our story.
She smiled.
Do I still deserve the couch?
Well, No…… But let's have some fun tonight, she
said.
Slowly our clothes were thrown at the corner.
Our mouths started to explore each other, I don't
know what happened, I fell asleep on her that night.

(46)

After a few years............

Hey Krissh, How are you, I asked?
A damn tired buddy, It was a long flight, he said.
Hey Isabelle, Where's the junior Krissh, I asked?
Well, he's here.
He looks just like you Krissh.
That's what everyone says, he said.

Where's Rahasya, he asked?
She's at home busy preparing for you guys, I said.
Let's go, I have arranged everything for you guys, I said.
I can have a hot shower, a good coffee, Isabelle said.

We reached home.
Rahasya came out running.
Awwww! he looks just like Krissh, she said.
I know, junior Krissh, she said.
What's your name junior, she asked?
My name is Harshavardhan and I'm 7 years old, he said.
You look, tall man, I said.
Just like his father, Isabelle said.
I laughed.

Alright come on, Le's get you guys freshed up, I said.
Hey by the way where's our queen, Isabelle asked?

She's in the shower, She will be out soon, Rahasya said.

Isabelle and Krissh got freshed up.
As Isabelle went inside the kitchen, she heard both of them playing.
Ah! He's already found his playmate, Isabelle said.
Yeah! come on let me introduce to Aurora, I said.
Aurora! That's a wonderful name, she said.
Hey kids, Hiiiiiiiiiiii, Isabelle said.
Hiiiii aunty, how are you, my father has told a lot about Krissh uncle and you, she said.
Oh really! she said.

What he has said to you, she asked?
How my father ended up with my mom, and how you guys helped my parents, she said.
That's nice of you. By the way Aurora, you have got a beautiful name, she said.
Thank you, aunty, she said.

Well, today we are going to do a bonfire and party hard in front of our house, I said.
Yaaaaaaaaaaaaaaaayyyyyyyyyyy! children's shouted with happiness.

It's been years, how's your work Rahul, Krissh asked?
It's going on good, gained a bit of fame and name, I said.
That's good. How about you Krissh, what's going on in India, I asked?
It's good buddy. It's the same stuff, he said.

Isabelle and Rahasya were at the kitchen getting dishes ready for the evening party.

I started the bonfire and we danced altogether.
Had snacks, got drunk. It was fun having such a good moment after years.
We were happy.

It was getting late.
Did junior sleep, Rahasya asked?
Yeah! he's an early riser, so he can't control his sleep, she said.
What about Aurora, Krissh asked?
I'll get her to bed now, It's time, Rahasya said.

No, I'll go, I said.
As I went up she was singing a song.
I opened the door, You didn't sleep, I asked?
No daddy, Am not sleepy yet, she said.
Well, am here, now get sleeping, I said.
I covered her with a blanket.
Nightlight, she said.
Yes, baby, I won't forget.

Love you, papa, she said.
Love you too baby, I said.
I kissed on her forehead, switched on the nightlight.
Before closing the door, I looked at her.
Yes, daddy, she asked?
Nothing baby, ***"you're the spitting image of my angel"***, I said.
Now sleep let's wake up early and enjoy the day with parties and stuff, I said.

She smiled at me and I closed the door.

When I turned back and I saw Rahasya looking at me with tears in her eyes.
She held my hand and walked across the room near the window. We looked Isabelle and Krissh sitting down at the fire.
She put her head on my shoulder and said.
I love you so much Rahul.
I smiled at her and Kissed on her forehead.
I love you too Ammu, I said.

Epilogue

After a year……..

I was staring at my laptop which was top of the desk.
My eyes were drowsy. I could see dreams while my eyes were half closed.
The coffee on the table was cold.
The clock's ticking was making me to go into the subconscious world.

Suddenly my phone rang. I looked at the time. It was 12:00 am.
Yes? This is Rahul.
The reception was bad. I could barely hear what the other person is saying. I could hear only half of the words.
THIS…………AN……………GENCY.
I'm not able to hear you, can you repeat..
HELLO…………

It's an emergency. Please come to the hospital immediately.
The call got disconnected.

I was so scared. I started to sweat.
Immediately I took my car and ran to the garage. I reversed my car and rushed to the hospital.
I parked down the car in front of the hospital.

I went inside. The receptionist was not there. There was a total silence. The lights in the passage started to go and off.

I felt spooky. As I approached the reception, there was a note on the notice board. "Rahul, please rush to the conference building."

Conference building is the place where meeting and small events are conducted. So that the hospital shouldn't be disturbed.

I ran towards the building. There was a cry. I was shit spooked.
I went inside the building and ran upstairs towards the conference room. I was standing in front of the door.
The shivering was enough to kill me. Chills went down my spine. I opened the door. It was pitch black.

I switched on the light next to the door.

SURPRISE!!!! They all yelled.

One of my colleague said, "Look at his face, He seemed like a ghost has been haunted him.

I smiled, Rahasya came forward.
"Happy birthday my baby", she said.
My daughter ran towards me. She gave me a hug.

All my colleagues came and wished me.

*Rahasya went to the middle of the stage. She took
the mic.*

*I have something to announce before the party
starts, she said.*

*Ladies and gentlemen, As It is a special occasion, I
want to announce that my hubby is been writing a
Novel since 8 months. Of course, the novel is based
on our love story. The Novel will be published very
soon.*
Everybody started to congratulate me.

One of my co-worker asked.
What's the title buddy?
I looked at my daughter.
Lift me up in the air, she said.
I lifted her up and she said.
"You're the spitting image of my angel."